THE JOURNALS

of

ELEANOR DRUSE

This Large Print Book carries the
Seal of Approval of N.A.V.H.

THE JOURNALS
of
ELEANOR DRUSE

*My Investigation
of the Kingdom Hospital
Incident*

ELEANOR DRUSE

Published in 2004 by arrangement with Hyperion, an imprint of
Buena Vista Books, Inc.

Wheeler Large Print Hardcover.

The text of this Large Print edition is unabridged.
Other aspects of the book may vary from the original edition.

Set in 16 pt. Plantin by Christina S. Huff.

Printed in the United States on permanent paper.

Library of Congress Control Number: 2004041252
ISBN 1-58724-670-8 (lg. print : hc : alk. paper)

THE JOURNALS

of

ELEANOR DRUSE

As the Founder/CEO of NAVH, the only national health agency solely devoted to those who, although not totally blind, have an eye disease which could lead to serious visual impairment, I am pleased to recognize Thorndike Press* as one of the leading publishers in the large print field.

Founded in 1954 in San Francisco to prepare large print textbooks for partially seeing children, NAVH became the pioneer and standard setting agency in the preparation of large type.

Today, those publishers who meet our standards carry the prestigious "Seal of Approval" indicating high quality large print. We are delighted that Thorndike Press is one of the publishers whose titles meet these standards. We are also pleased to recognize the significant contribution Thorndike Press is making in this important and growing field.

Lorraine H. Marchi, L.H.D.
Founder/CEO
NAVH

* Thorndike Press encompasses the following imprints: Thorndike, Wheeler, Walker and Large Print Press.

FOREWORD

COVER LETTER TO STEPHEN KING

Dear Mr. King:

I am writing to you because I know from reading your books that you are a true believer in the world of spirits, that you had a near-death experience similar to mine, and because you are a fellow Mainer.

My name is Eleanor Sarah Druse, Sally to my friends. I am seventy-five years of age, born 2 November 1928, All Souls' Day, at the old Kingdom Hospital in the town of Lewiston, Maine, where I have lived most of my life. Although I am a trained experimental psychologist and professor emeritus of noetic sciences and esoteric psychology at Lewiston's Faust College, I cannot at this early date write with the authority and detachment of a scientist working in a controlled environment. My research into the baffling and disturbing events I have witnessed at Kingdom Hospital is so far unfunded and has of necessity been conducted in the

7

field, where I have done my best to describe breaking events in uncontrolled, even chaotic circumstances.

I do not have the necessary staff and equipment to conduct more rigorous, definitive studies, but I believe that I have collected tangible evidence of what we psychologists call a "sensed presence" at Lewiston's Kingdom Hospital. I believe this to be the distressed spirit of a child who has repeatedly made herself known to me (throughout my life) and who, for reasons still unknown, is unable to pass beyond what the great Swedish mystic Emanuel Swedenborg called the First State after death. I intend to find out who this poor child was in life, what happened to her, and if I can, how to help her find eternal rest, but I am opposed in my endeavors by powerful adversaries with vested interests to protect.

Although I lack the funding to conduct the necessary scientific research, I have tried to write this account with the objectivity and accuracy of a careful and ethical journalist. When appropriate, I have also described my own subjective impressions, because as you will see, on many occasions the child makes herself present only to me. I don't know if the child has chosen me as a medium and vessel for her distress, or if her grief is aimless and I sense her voice only because of my own clairaudient aptitudes.

I apologize for sending handwritten notebooks, but I have no secretary or assistant, and I write in haste during the press of events leading up to my investigation of the sensed presence at Kingdom Hospital. If these pages speak to you, Mr. King, and if you have a secretary or typist at your disposal who could take on the work of typing these notes, I would be so grateful. My hope is that a typed manuscript could be submitted to the National Association for the Scientific Investigation of Claims of the Paranormal and other organizations devoted to rigorously examining claims of extrasensory perception, parapsychology, precognition, and psychokinesis.

Please read these pages as an introduction only to what I believe will one day be a complete scientific study and assessment of the remarkable occurrences witnessed by myself and others at Kingdom Hospital beginning in December of the year 2002 and continuing to the present time.

Mr. King, I am seventy-five years old — still vigorous and alert — but I have also had disquieting premonitions that my struggle to learn the secrets of this girl's distressed spiritual exile may lead to my own death. If I must shed this heavy flesh and cross the barrier to the beyond, then let my written words live on after me and speak for me when I am gone from this world. I have also included a detailed summary of my medical condition, because my nemesis is a physician whose weapon of choice is diagnosis.

If anything happens to me, and if subsequent research proves that the girl's spirit is still abandoned, confused, and suffering, then please find someone to help her. As you will see in the papers I have en-

closed, she can indeed be reached, and in time I believe that she will be able to tell us why she cannot rest.

God be with us all,

Most sincerely, and with great admiration for your work,

Eleanor Druse

THY KINGDOM COME

THE PAST PHONES HOME

On December thirteenth of the year 2002, I was awakened in the wee-hour stillness of a winter's night by my ringing telephone. At that hour, especially at my age, phone calls often amount to progress reports from the angel of death, whose duties include making unscheduled house calls in the dead of night and filling the obituaries with the names of my elderly friends. I expected that this was just such a call and was surprised to hear my son's voice instead.

Bobby works the night shift as an orderly at Kingdom Hospital here in Lewiston, Maine. He was calling from work, and I thought it might be about one of the hospice patients I visit from time to time. I do some volunteer work on Kingdom Hospital's sunshine ward. I go in once a week or so; I sit with the dying and make their final days less lonely, hold their hands, pray with them, read Swedenborg or William Blake to them — anything to help them make ready for

11

their grand journeys. If they are adventurers or spiritualists, then I'm happy to be of service with my crystals, cards, or runes, or even with a séance if they are anxious to reach a friend or family member.

Once in a great while I have had a call from the sunshine ward at night, especially if the patient was a close friend or if I had grown fond of the family during their visits. But I sensed that this was something else again.

"Mum," said Bobby, "sorry to wake you, but we got something strange going on here."

Bobby is not often roused to action, and making a phone call at this hour was, for him, tantamount to a dramatic exploit, maybe even aerobic exercise. In the Middle Ages, when the genius doctors all thought our temperaments were ruled by the four cardinal humors — blood, black bile, yellow bile, and phlegm — Bobby would have been diagnosed as phlegmatic. These days I think they call it sensory integration disorder or amotivational syndrome. He's a good boy, but a perversely willful underachiever. He isn't quite forty years old yet, so I'm still looking out for signs of progress. Be assured that Bobby calling at 2:57 A.M. on a winter's night meant that something far beyond strange was afoot.

"What is it, Bobby? Are you at the hospital? What's wrong?"

"Mum, there's an attempted suicide here. A Mrs. Madeline Kruger. I think we know the family. She's fairly gaga, Mum. Failing all of her cranial checks: doesn't quite know what she's doing, how old she is, where she lives. When the nurses asked her who's the president, she said Franklin Delano Roosevelt. When they asked her what year is it, she said 1939."

"Madeline Kruger?" I repeated the name and felt a cold mass congeal in my solar plexus and spread to my arms and legs on a cresting wave of gooseflesh. I shivered and caught my breath. I assumed that my visceral reactions were all caused by the nature of the call. Attempted suicide? I'd known Madeline Kruger (maiden name Jensen) since childhood — we were the same age — but I hadn't seen or heard from her in twenty . . . hold on, could be thirty years, at least. Lloyd Kruger had run off and left her with nothing but his last name and three kids a long time ago — roughly the same decade my ex-husband left me.

"What's happened to her? Did she tell you to call me?"

"It's weirder than that, Mum. She keeps using your name. Sally this and Sally that. And when the nurses asked her, 'Who's Sally?' she said, 'Why, little Sally Druse, of course.' "

I felt the same cold mass expand inside me again and tried to think why in heaven Madeline Kruger would suddenly be invoking my name after I exchanged pleasantries with her in the produce section nearly thirty years ago, and why just after she attempted to take her own life? I sat up and tried to clear my head, because I seemed to be on the verge of remembering something she'd told me, some terrible confession she'd sworn me to secrecy over when we were still children. Maybe I'd forgotten it on purpose, so I couldn't tell anybody.

"She's still woozy, Mum, from gas and pills. They don't seem to be able to find any family or next of kin."

"She needs me, then, doesn't she, Bobby?"

"The other thing is," he said, "she left a note. A long one."

I felt cold all over again and shivered.

"It has your name in it, Mum."

"Well, what does it say?"

"They won't show it to me, Mum. They just said she mentions you in her note. They asked me to call you, because she's still talking about you. Something about tell Sally Druse the little girl is still here or the little girl is coming back. Are you sure you didn't work with Mrs. Kruger on the sunshine ward? Or read her fortune somewhere? You didn't cast any spells on her or anything, did you?"

"Bobby, I don't cast spells, and I haven't spoken to Madeline Kruger in thirty years. But I want to see her now."

"Well, look out the window, Mum. We've had two feet of snow since yesterday. Stay home. Don't go out. Turn on the TV and the weather alert will tell you the same."

Bobby said that the side streets were snowpack and the main thoroughfares black ice, and that under no circumstances should I try to come to the hospital. Too dangerous. Mrs. Kruger's stomach had been pumped (pills, too!), so she probably wouldn't recover enough to receive visitors until morning, at which time Bobby promised he would come home and drive me in his truck to see her.

I told Bobby that he was absolutely right, that I dared not go out, and that I would wait for him to pick me up in the morning. Then I hung up the phone, went out to the garage, started my old Volvo, and drove to Kingdom Hospital so I could be with poor Madeline on the darkest night of her life. Bobby is something of a lummox in these matters, especially if he thought I could roll over and go back to sleep after learning that a childhood friend of mine was alone in the world, locked up in a psych ward, and still tormented by whatever demons had pursued her to the brink of self-slaughter.

There was a full moon that dread night in December, and the roads looked like bobsled runs, with snow heaped on either side to form a half tunnel out of which I could not see. I drove ten miles an hour the whole way, feeling guilty for all of the good I hadn't done Madeline for the last third of a century, and remembering as much as I could about her.

We had been close friends when we were little girls, and I do remember our being in the hospital together when we were ten or eleven years old. The doctors said it was whooping cough, but my mother blamed the Androscoggin River, which in those days was used as a sewer for untreated paper-mill effluents, and the fumes were rumored to peel the paint off houses and burn the lungs of children. "That's the smell of money," the locals used to say. Whatever the diagnosis, Madeline and I missed a week or so of school, bedridden in that old bandage hotel, which burned to the ground not long after they let us out of there.

After that, we grew apart: Madeline went to St. Dominic's; I went to Lewiston High. Then I went to the University of Maine at Orono and completely lost track of her, but I heard later that she had been an academic star at Vassar — a philosophy or theology major, if I recall. I studied parapsychology and psi phenomena abroad in Europe for five years before I moved back to Lewiston and took an appointment in the psychology department here at Faust College. Madeline also moved back, but she apparently didn't want to teach or go to graduate school. She stayed home and cared for Lloyd's children. I heard she was working on a novel and had had a short story or two published in literary magazines.

I saw her once or twice in our forties, I think. I remember us commiserating because we had both had the misfortune of being discarded by husbands who, at midlife, changed us out for newer models and left us to raise fatherless children. The story was an old, boring one, even then. I had only Bobby to look after when my husband, Randall — like me, he was a professor at Faust College — ran off with one of his art history students. Madeline's boy and her two girls were still in grade school when her husband took off. The gossips on the beauty shop circuit said that Lloyd Kruger fell for a divorced real estate agent with a 38-inch bust, who apparently showed him more than a house one day. That was back in, oh, the early seventies at least, but I also recall coming across Madeline once or twice after her divorce, and it was as if the darkness visible had fallen like a shroud behind her eyes, and all of those educated smarts were going to waste in there with nobody home to turn on the lights.

Later I heard from friends of mutual friends that she had struggled with depression and eating and anxiety disorders; that she'd been on a rotating regimen of antidepressants and electroshock therapies. I always meant to call and see how she was doing. Then they doubled my course load at Faust, and Bobby kept growing up, and pretty soon Madeline and I were separated by decades.

Her melancholy must have fed on the travails of old age until it fattened to suicidal despair. As I made my way over those icy roads, I charged myself with a mission: to be there at Madeline's bedside and welcome her back to

17

this world after her determined attempt to leave it.

I followed a caravan of trucks and snowplows to Kingdom Hospital and parked in the doctors' lot, which was almost empty. They had the lots all plowed out, but I noticed that the walkway outside the emergency room was treacherous. I had to hold on to the handrail for dear life and shuffle my way to the door like a penguin on skates.

Bobby is good friends with Otto, the security guard, and I found the two of them drinking coffee in Otto's cubicle just off the ER entrance. Otto's eyes are failing behind Coke-bottle glasses, and Bobby sometimes watches the monitors for him; no harm done, and the night shift supervisor thinks of it as reasonable accommodation of Otto's visual handicap. Otto also has a dog, Blondi, a German shepherd who helps him get around and sleeps under the security console, where I could see him gnawing on a rawhide toy.

Bobby hid his pipe and his tobacco pouch. An odious habit! His teeth and gums were orange from the poison. He was miffed about my driving, but what could he say? There I was: living proof that I could make the drive without incident. Before I could be seen with him, I had to tidy him up. His hair stood out every which way and his shirt was untucked, making him look even heavier. I sent him into the men's room with a comb and a toothbrush, and wished something could be done about his shoes, the heels of which had broken down from his walking on them.

He came out, one side of his hair soaked and mashed against the side of his head and the other sticking up like stalks of winter wheat. He walked with me to the elevators, groaning while I hacked away at his hair with the comb. He decided to ride with me, because if nobody was in the psych nurses' station I wouldn't even be able to get in the place.

I pinned on my hospice worker ID badge so I would look somewhat official, and up we went to the Kingdom Hospital psychiatric ward.

I'd been a patient on the orthopedic ward and the neurology ward before — for arthritis, tinnitus, some gastric reflux — the usual repairs and servicing the human body requires once the seventy-year limited warranty runs out. I'd never been to the psychiatric ward, though I once worked with a lady in hospice, a schizophrenic who'd been transferred to us from psychiatry. She used to whisper in my ear, "Don't tell nobody else but the doctor says I caught that shishtofraynia bug that's going around."

The elevator stopped and we stepped out into a secure waiting area outside of a well-lit nurses' station, the upper half of which was enclosed on all four sides by steel mullions and chicken-wire safety glass.

A lone nurse was on the telephone, chart open in front of her. She glanced at Bobby and me and smiled, while Bobby opened the door into the station with a key on a chain.

The nurse pointed at a coffeepot, but we shook our heads. Her name tag said LAUREL WERLING, R.N.

"She had the ipecac only," said the nurse into the phone. "Dr. Hook didn't want her to have anything else because he was afraid of interactions with other drugs she may have taken that we don't know about."

While we waited, I looked around the nurses' station, which was like none other I'd seen in the Kingdom. Each wall of the quadrangle had a thick dead-bolted wooden door with a little hinged windowpane of chicken-wire glass set into it at eye level. Three of the bolted doors gave out into separate dark hallways, lit at this hour only by exit signs glowing fire-engine red at the far ends. The fourth door opened into the waiting area we'd entered from, and Bobby had bolted it after us.

I looked through the darkened glass and out onto the ward, where an emaciated elderly man in a frayed and dirty hospital gown appeared out of the darkness in the hallway opposite like an apparition taking shape in a graveyard, gradually becoming visible as he drifted toward the fluorescent lights of the nurses' station. He stopped in front of the bolted wooden door, his head framed by the inset pane of wired glass, his skull plainly visible under papery hairless, age-spotted flesh. He had a livid ropy scar on the left side of his head that zigzagged like a lightning bolt from his temple all the way behind his ear. I kept feeling I was on the verge of recognizing him, as if I'd known him as a much younger man or seen a photo of him somewhere: William Burroughs from the *Naked Lunch* jacket? The mortician who'd buried my mother and father at the Oak Lawn Funeral Home?

Behind him on the wall was a fire alarm.

In case of fire, break glass, I thought. It didn't say that anywhere on or near the alarm, and it wasn't that kind of fire alarm, because you can't have glass anywhere out on the psychiatric ward itself. I don't know why I thought it. I just did.

He raised his bony hand and rapped on the door of the nurses' station with his knuckles.

The nurse kept talking into the phone while she opened the hatch in the door and handed out a small paper cup of pills and another with a swallow's worth of water in it.

Glaring at me, the old man took the pills and the water and said, "You wanna know what love is?"

I don't know why, but his question raised gooseflesh all over my body. I shuddered in the grip of a violent chill.

The nurse made a face and turned sharply away from the old guy, as if she'd had enough of him weeks ago. She stuck a finger in her open ear and pressed the handset against her other one. "I'm sorry," she said into the phone, "say again?"

"I said, Do you wanna know what love is?" the old man in the gown repeated loudly.

I gasped and stared at him. I *knew* him. The priest from St. Dymphna's they'd arrested for child abuse? No, but . . .

The nurse waved him off and continued her phone conversation.

The old guy tossed the pills into the back of his mouth, followed with the water, and gulped. He crumpled the paper cups and balled them up, one in each fist.

"It's pigs in a litter lying close together to keep warm."

He glowered at me as if he was waiting for me to argue with him.

"I'll say a prayer for you," I offered. "God bless you."

"Blessed are the young," he said, "for they shall inherit the national debt. Did you know that God is really three persons — Father, Son, and Holy Spirit — who are united in one substance or being, kind of like a lite beer that tastes great but is also less filling, and makes the whores of Babylon mud-wrestle in the streets."

He barked a mirthless laugh, turned, and trudged back down the hallway, his gown open in the back, the sallow cheeks of his skinny buttocks drooping and puckering as he walked away into the darkness.

In case of fire, break glass.

"Still no luck reaching any family," the nurse said into the phone. Then she glanced at me, smiled, and said, "But Mrs. Druse is here. She may be able to tell us something."

Bobby's beeper sounded, just about the time Nurse Werling got off the phone. He looked down at it and grumbled about having to transport someone from the emergency room.

"Mum, you come down to Otto's cubicle when you're finished, you hear? I don't want you driving home in this, you understand?"

"I love you, Bobby," I said.

"Love you, too, Mum," he mumbled.

Laurel Werling was a pleasant woman, but she acted even younger than she looked and seemed a trifle inexperienced, as if she was used to being second in command to someone who had the night off. She made several more phone calls to make sure she was handling Madeline Kruger's attempted suicide according to protocols. I learned that the police had found Madeline in her kitchen, where she had extinguished the pilot light on her stove, turned on the gas, put a pillow in the oven, and laid her head on it. They'd also found an empty bottle of pain medication on the counter.

Nurse Werling explained that Madeline was uncooperative and unable or unwilling to provide information the hospital needed to reach her family or next of kin. Madeline seemed disoriented as to time and place, and to have regressed to a childish recalcitrance. The only name that came up reliably in her conversations so far was mine.

I agreed to help any way I could, but I confessed to Ms. Werling that although I had spent
many hours sitting with the dying on the sunshine ward, I had no experience dealing with
suicidal patients. I knew enough of human nature to suspect that Madeline might not exactly
be thrilled to have survived her brush with
death. She would wake up knowing that in the
end she had failed even at failing, had botched
the last thing she had to do right. Otherwise I
had no idea what to expect, what to say or do.

Ms. Werling said I should follow Madeline's
lead and let her talk about whatever she wished.
She said that attempted suicides often express
anger and bitterness against loved ones, which
she hoped might give us an opening to obtain
contact information for her son and her daughters, or at least determine what cities they were
living in.

The nurse led me out into the same hallway
where that cranky old rawbones in a gown had
appeared. Indeed, I could see him down at the
far end of the hallway, backlit by the bluish glow
of a *Happy Days* rerun, poking through an ash-
tray in search of butts, from the looks of it.

Our footsteps echoed on the marble flooring,
but the old one never so much as looked our way.

The corridor was lined with more thick
wooden doors, some bolted shut, some opening
into darkness.

Midway down the hall, an unshaven middle-
aged man in an orderly's uniform very like the

one Bobby wears was sitting outside a room in a comfortable recliner, a can of Nozz-A-La cola on the table next to him. He had a book open in his lap and a gooseneck lamp pulled up alongside, but his chin had settled on his chest, and it was obvious he had dozed off.

"That's Angelo Charron," said the nurse, raising her voice as we approached, probably because she didn't want to discipline the orderly for sleeping on the job. "Mrs. Kruger is on suicide precautions, which means someone must keep her in plain view at all times."

She cleared her throat, and Mr. Charron jerked awake in his chair.

"This is Mrs. Druse," the nurse said. "Sally Druse. She's a family friend."

"Good morning, sir," I said, and shook his hand.

I caught the fruity scent of alcohol on his breath, despite his attempt to speak out of the far side of his mouth.

"Morning, ma'am," he said. He did his best to look alert and steered the lamplight away from his red eyes.

I looked into the dark room for some sign of Madeline.

The orderly guided the dim beam of his reading light carefully into the darkness, first finding the foot of the bed and then slowly ascending to reveal the silhouette of the patient's feet under the bedding. The head of the bed was raised and facing us, but shrouded in darkness.

"She's been asleep for an hour or so," he said softly, "but she's restless. If you stick around she'll probably wake up and start talking about you and the little girl again."

"What little girl?" I asked.

He shrugged. "She's not making much sense. Why don't you have a listen and see if you can tell what she's talking about?"

The nurse and I went ahead of the beam and into the room, and just as we did so, Mr. Charron's shaky hand must have lost its grip on the lamp cover, for the beam of its light fell full onto Mrs. Kruger's torso and face.

On earth as it is in hell, may I never see such a death's-head again. Madeline's face was locked open in a rictus of stark terror, staring straight ahead as if into damnation's gate. Her gaping mouth and bulging eyes left no doubt about whether it's possible to literally die of fright. Some ghastly specter like the basilisks of old had killed her with a glance. Her head was thrown back, her palms up, open as if to receive the stigmata, which she had apparently inflicted with an ice pick, still loosely held in one bloody hand.

Nurse Werling and I cried out and came near death ourselves, shaking, unable to breathe. We clutched at each other like scared little girls and held on, afraid one of us might run away and leave the other alone in this chamber with such a frightful corpse.

There was another more terrifying complication.

The wound she'd made in her throat gaped open like a second mouth, and boiling from that ugly gash were seething masses of black ants. Ants had likewise erupted from the gashes in her wrists and had eaten away the edges of her skin, streaming furiously in and out of her suppurating wounds, as if the entirety of her lifeless body had been colonized by vast swarming black armies.

I heard harsh laughter coming in from the hallway.

I knew that voice. It was the old man who'd come for his pills at the nurses' station.

Do you wanna know what love is?

NEAR DEATH

PILLARS OF SALT

When human intelligence is suddenly confronted by the supernatural, death (the purest of all epiphanies) may be instantaneous. Certain prodigies, wonders, abominations, monstrosities, freaks of nature, angels, demons, and other supernatural leaks into the material world are too much for us mere mortals to see. Such were Medusa and the serpent-haired gorgons Aeschylus wrote of, whom none could look upon without perishing. If we do not avert our eyes in time, we die.

Sometimes instead of dying instantly from fright or shock, we may survive the initial horror and astonishment, only to slowly waste away in the thrall of some terrible or numinous image burned onto the faceplate of memory, a single fixed idea. Beauty only the first touch of terror we can still bear, and all that. The great Borges wrote of the Zahir, which in Arabic means notorious and visible (one of the ninety-nine names of God). In Muslim countries, the Zahir also refers to beings or things that possess the terrible quality of being unforgettable and whose image finally drives people mad. It's as if the Zahir or some other unforgettable fiend infects the mind with a frightful fixation more hideous than its original shape, and memory suckles it along to a fatal obsession that in the end turns and devours the mind that fed it. Death comes because we forsake the entire universe for one autochthonous idea.

Madeline Kruger's ant-infested corpse dealt me just such a mortal, visionary blow. I gave up the ghost right there in the room, I guess. My knees gave out, my feet flew east, I fell west, and the back of my head smacked the marble floor.

Flat on my back, I looked up into the stark ceiling tiles and dead light fixtures and panicked: *my hip!* At my age, a firing squad is preferable to a shattered hip, and all the Fosamax in the world won't protect you. *If my hip is fractured, please make my bed in the grave, thank you very much. Amen.*

My half-formed death wish almost came true, and I watched, helpless, as blackness constricted my vision and squeezed out the visible world. I tumbled backward, like Alice falling down the rabbit hole, but only for a second. The next thing I knew, I was somewhere up near the ceiling tiles looking down and watching them call a code blue on yours truly.

Frankly, expiring right there on the floor was

fine by me. I certainly didn't want to die at home and haunt my own house. I wanted Bobby to have the place and not be vexed by the memory of finding me dead in one room or another; *if my time is up, so be it,* I thought.

I watched all the personnel bowing over my body and speaking to each other: "She's unresponsive." "Do we have a pulse?" "She's not breathing." "Is she gone?" I have a clear memory of being outside and above myself, looking down and seeing the code blue team come in with that cart full of tools and equipment. I love medical technology, and it was a delight to have a bird's-eye view of it being deployed so earnestly to rescue me. I felt strangely detached about the outcome of the procedures. I was of two minds about whether to try and will myself back into that old arthritic bag of bones. Could I get an update on the hip first?

I saw the nurses and medical residents running needles and tubes into my arms, injecting me with drugs, giving me oxygen by mask. I recall being skeptical about whether all of this would do any good. Then dark fur crowded around my shrinking tunnel vision. I had the peculiar sensation of settling back down on the mattress of myself for a long winter's nap.

Here it comes, I thought. *The undiscovered country. The big show. The end of all plots. The cure for all diseases. The leap in the night.*

May I have the last dance alone?

THE GOOD

Being dead was the best thing that ever happened to me. Death was better than the book, better than the movie, better than all those philosophical speculations and theological revelations I'd read about in college. Too bad there was no way to send back word to all of those insipid flatlanders who think that the human soul is nothing more than static given off by brain cells. Alert! Incoming from freshly dead Sally Druse: You materialists are sorely mistaken.

Instead of the Big Nothing, I was pleased to discover an afterlife of deliciously dreamless eternal rest. It was too dark to tell if I had a body, but if I did, it felt as if I were submerged and drifting in a vast starless sea of warm black amniotic fluid. Not a care disturbed me, and I seemed to have just enough sightless awareness to enjoy the bliss of suspended animation without the unpleasantness of actual cognition. For the first time, here or hereafter, being was effortless; uncomplicated by memory, apprehension, guilt, loneliness, or pain. All the restorative benefits of deep sleep were mine, with none of the nightmares or waking fears — just an endless slow-motion falling through deep space to the sea of tranquility.

By some miracle, I was able to revel in this beatific state without quite being conscious of it. Instead, I seemed always on the verge of thinking, without ever rupturing the limen of what my philosophy professors had called apperception — the mental act in which the mind becomes aware of itself perceiving. Let that old Greek pederast Socrates prattle on about how the unreflective life is not worth living. This was unreflection at its finest, and it was a garden of vegetable raptures compared with the life I'd lived on earth.

Then I felt the tingle of a memory trace — Madeline Kruger and the little girl — and it was almost as if I'd wrecked it all by enjoying it. Had I somehow stepped outside of the delicious mindlessness of the afterlife by savoring it?

Sensations followed. My dreamy half-executed velleities became full-blown volitions. I moved an eyelid, then a finger, and then the unspeakable horror of consciousness loomed on the horizon like a gathering thunderhead.

Mother of Mary, I was headed back! Maybe the heat lightning of awareness flickering in the distance was just my leftover cortical static. Maybe if I kept my eyes closed and was careful not to breathe or move, I could slip back under the waves and descend again into that warm infinite blackness, forever.

But no. I bobbed and resurfaced. I heard sounds — beeping noises, rhythmic hissing, voices. Air filled my lungs, even when I tried not to breathe. Unwanted mental events kept disturbing my aimless reveries of death. For instance, if I was remembering things such as Madeline Kruger and apperception, didn't that mean my brain was still working? Still with me? And the ants roiling in poor Madeline's wounds! I remembered them, which might mean I had a brain to remember them with? What if I was keeping my eyes closed by a sheer act of will, which meant that I had eyelids and willpower, which meant . . . alas.

THE BAD

Another beep, more rhythmic hissing, voices. Then the cardinal symptom of mortal consciousness: pain. A headache, one bad enough to prove I had a head, same as a watch proves a watchmaker. If pain was part of the ambience, I should hurry back to the land of the living, because if the rumors were true, an afterlife headache could last forever and a day.

The back of my eyelids were indigo veined in bloodred — the color of a pregnant night sky ready to deliver a thunderstorm. I allowed them to slit open. What I saw might be heaven or hell, but if so, it was camouflaged as an intensive care unit.

Gowned and hooded figures hurried and bowed over me under bright lights. They carried sacramental vessels and chanted in Latin. A warlock with an ornamental headdress leaned over me with a weapon.

"That's V-fib," he said through a sacred mask. "Defibrillator! Paddles!"

So the bastard was going to spank me with a paddle.

Whoa! There I was back up on the ceiling again, looking down at the top of his covered head bowing over my flabby whiteness. Spank me with a paddle now, you beast. See if I care.

I was all the way out of body again. That's right, and I knew a lot about near-death experiences. I'd read about them.

A low roar seemed to reverberate somewhere deep within my newly disembodied state (impossible, I know, the bewildering sensation of emptiness vibrating). The roar grew louder and seemed to bear me aloft, as if I were a hawk gyring in a thermal, but instead of soaring through cumulus clouds and empyrean blue, I was hurtling upward in a dark concrete passage made of stained cinder blocks and rusty tie-rods. I was rising toward a light at the top of it. When I looked down, I saw that I was ascending in an elevator shaft. Beneath me I could see descending elevator cars — cages, really, suspended by cables — crowded with people waving their arms, clawing at one another, reaching up to me, trying to escape, beseeching me, crying mercy. But the elevator cars continued their descent, down to where shadows warred with flames in the infernal depths far below.

I looked up again at the white radiance and continued rising toward it. I heard a voice calling to me from inside the light, and I sensed an ineffable presence, which seemed to be calling me toward it and reeling me in with tendrils of delicate light.

It was like reading a script for a schlocky TV movie called *Sally Druse and the Light at the End of the Dark Tunnel.* I have extensively studied what psychologists and neuroscientists in my field refer to as out-of-body experiences (OBE) and near-death experiences (NDE). In the 1980s I thoroughly researched the phenomena with Dr. Susan Blackmore, at the University of Surrey in England. So having such an experience myself made me feel like a psychiatrist stretching out on another analyst's couch. Even while it was happening to me, I recalled thinking that except for a few idiosyncratic particulars, my afterlife interlude seemed to consist of an infinite cliché.

I wish I could report that I met the spirits of friends and relatives who had passed on before me and were eager to lead me toward the light, where a voice communicated with me telepathically, showed me the instant replay of my life on earth, and told me that I had nothing to fear because: All Is Well in the Hereafter, Sally Druse, Now and Forever, Amen.

Instead, as I drew near the radiance at the apex of the passage, the voice became distressed and the light slowly died, like the glow of an ember being soaked up by an absorbent blackness so vast and deep it glistened; as if I — a being of light — were about to be sucked inside a dark star or an obsidian crystal. I felt the same ineffable presence and heard it sigh in the smoldering ash.

The rushing abruptly stopped and gave way to a soundless void. The voice called out, and again I seemed to feel the timbre of its desperation resonate inside my newly incorporeal self.

It was the cry of a child, a little girl, whose inarticulate pleas were so forlorn and piteous it anguished me almost to bursting, for I had no tears or eyes to weep them. I suspect that no living writer commands a vocabulary capable of describing the voice I heard at the top of that elevator shaft, so where do I begin? The misery articulated in that pathetic cry was distinctly human, yet it was not of this world. That cry harrowed me with visions of what lay beyond the dying light: a kingdom of perpetual night, where death and darkness are the only lights, and the sightless damned cried out their fright. Somewhere in that sunless ocean clotted with nightmares a child was lost and alone. Though it seemed like a century ago, I remembered what the orderly with alcohol on his breath had said just before I'd left the world: "If you stick around she'll probably wake up and start talking about you and the little girl again."

I heard a bell ringing. A chime perhaps, or just a tinkling handbell of the sort used in the last century to summon the household to tea.

What little girl?

THE UGLY

By the last feeble rays of the smoldering cinders, I saw (with what spectral sense organs, I don't know) a creature standing guard at the top of the shaft, where the opening gave out into perpetual night. I could make out only his silhouette in the penumbral shadows: the head of giant jackal or anteater, the torso and body half man, half beast. Teeth glistened once and disappeared in the dark. Again I heard the distressing cries of the child — not words or speech, only lamentations, which seemed to express a century's worth of loneliness and despair.

The child's cry moved me to pity, but also to unspeakable dread that the creature guarding the gate should give me passage to a similar fate.

I looked down where the elevator cages had descended miles below the earth.

More chimes, bells ringing. Then I heard something beeping, as if terrorists had planted bombs somewhere in the shaft, and it was only a matter of seconds before the timers triggered the blasts and engulfed the passage in flames.

I was struck by lightning and opened my eyes under blinding artificial lights.

THE REIGN OF SCIENCE

HIGH PRIEST OF THE GORILLAS

I couldn't tell if it was morning or night, because I seemed to be in a pod with no windows to the outside and big drum lights shining down from above. I had a plastic pipe in my throat, held in place by a collar of some kind, and every five seconds or so a machine hissed and inflated me as if I were a beached blowfish. I was hemmed in on both sides by steel railings that reminded me of the cattle gates I'd seen out in the puckerbush on my Uncle Mort's farm when I was a little girl. Everything smelled of alcohol and plastic, and my mouth tasted like medicinal lemon.

A pretty, thirtyish nurse in a gown and sterile gloves moved around my bed tending to electronic boxes on poles, and these gizmos were hooked up to me by tubes with fluid in them. I'd never seen her before, didn't know where I was or how long I'd been there. I tried to talk, which made the plastic pipe in my throat buckle, but no sound came out. I couldn't even grunt to get the nurse's attention. I tried to reach out and touch her elbow, but my wrists were tied to the bed with soft restraints.

I saw a small group of men and women in white lab coats — doctors? — but recognized not one of them. They were gathering outside my . . . was it a room? Not quite. More like a display case with glass windows, where I was to be a specimen, sick in bed, gagged by a pipe in my throat, and exhibited half naked in my hospital gown for any rubbernecker who walked by and wanted to take a gander at a bare-assed old lady with a bad headache.

In came the doctors wearing badges and ceremonial stethoscopes hanging around their necks like amulets. A big one with wavy hair swaggered out in front and seemed to be in charge. As the formation approached, they reminded me of a band of gorillas: a dominant male, followed by one or two subdominant males, followed by several mature females, followed by callow, fresh-faced youngsters.

The big one spoke first.

"I'm Dr. Stegman," he said, then indicated the doctor trailing his right elbow. "And this is Dr. Metzger."

Dr. Metzger was stocky but prissy, with manicured fingernails and a carefully arranged flap of hair combed over his pattern baldness. If I had to guess, his primary qualification for his subdominant role was that he was half a foot shorter than the silverback in charge.

Both doctors smiled.

Where's my son, Bobby?

"*Metzger* is German for butcher," said Stegman, "but please don't hold that against him."

The acolytes all smiled and shook their heads: *No, he's not a butcher. He's Dr. Metzger.*

It occurred to me that there had been an afterlife mix-up and I had inadvertently been sent to hell.

"Dr. Metzger is a psychiatrist. The rest of us are neurologists or neurosurgeons, with a few medical surgical people filling in the back rows," said Stegman. "Dr. Metzger will be in charge of the inorganic and the intangible, and we brain specialists will deal with the organic and the medical."

A tight smile my way. "Clear?"

Where's my son? Who made you my doctor?

This Stegman fellow wasn't talking to me so much as he was performing for the group — and I had no choice but to suck on my tube and be a mute straight man for his preening insolence.

"You had a close call there, young lady," said Stegman.

He pooched his lips and walked around my bed. His hair had been blown dry into an airbrushed confection that floated regally above his head like a scented halo.

"The next time you fall, madam, I'd do it on a softer floor."

He winked at me.

I pointed at the tube in my mouth and tried to talk again, which prompted a paternal smile from him and knowing looks from his followers. He marched back around to the foot of my bed, flaunting his own rude good health.

"Don't try to talk around that tube. That goes between your vocal cords and into your lungs so that the machine can breathe for you. You can't talk while that's in there."

No shit. But I don't want a machine doing my breathing for me, thank you very much.

Probably just as well I couldn't talk, as young people are often shocked when the elderly swear freely. Maybe someone could take the goddamn pipe out? Plus, as I learned later, a foul mouth is a common symptom of an acute temporal lobe injury.

One of the mature females in the band started putting films and pictures onto a lighted box on the wall.

"Now let's have a look," said Stegman, using a pointer to give the acolytes a tour of brain scans with my name on them.

"Mrs. Drusey here slips on the ice or whatever, giving herself a contra coup injury, resulting in contusion and hemorrhage in her right temporal lobe. The description of Kluver-Bucy-like syndrome? Anybody?" He looked around. "Nobody? I thought so. Any Korsakoff's psychosis?"

I have to admit, I love it when they take pictures of my brain. I wished I could have been awake for those! Something so exciting about those great omniscient devices seeing deep inside, where no eye has seen and no light has shined.

He moved his pointer again to another scan and indicated a dot.

"And what about this delightful little enigma right here in the left frontal lobe? If it's malignant, it's brand new. If it's not brand new, is it a low-grade tumor? A cyst? Sclerosis from a tiny stroke or previous trauma? Whatever it is, it presents a fascinating teaser: Did it *cause* the fall or is it just an incidental finding after the fact? Did they send us any historical scans on her?"

I made writing motions with my right hand and pointed to the pad and pen on my writing table.

The nurse held the pad for me so I could write: (*1*) *Where is my son, Bobby?* (*2*) *Is this Kingdom Hospital in Lewiston, Maine?*

Stegman had gone back to conferring about shadows and hot spots on pretty scans and stringing Latin words together like Legos.

"Your son, Bobby, is here," said the nurse. "He went to get something to eat. He's coming right back. My name is Claudia."

The nurse smiled. She seemed kind and capable, but before she could continue, the pad attracted the attention of Dr. Stegman, who found my second question so ludicrous it moved him to antic good humor, which touched off devotional merriment in his followers.

"Lewiston, Maine?" he repeated. "Madam, this is Boston General Medical Center. One of the top five medical centers in the United States. And while Maine is not too far away as the crow flies, I assure you that *medically speaking*, Maine is *nowhere near* Boston, Massachusetts. You won't find the like of these physicians in Lewisport, Maine."

Boston? How in the world . . . ?

Good humor all around, and nobody was too concerned about whether the little spot on the scan was a malignancy. After all, it wasn't a picture of their brain, it was a picture of mine. These intelligent primates were members of the science tribe. I was well acquainted with their customs and rituals. Scientists could be useful now and then, but I always took care to deal with them at arm's length, for they are notoriously untrustworthy.

The woman doctor who put the scan images up took them down, and Dr. Stegman put his hand on the bedrail.

"If all goes well, that tube will be out this afternoon and we can talk. Then we'll take some more pictures and see what's going on inside that nut of yours. Okay?"

I frowned and motioned for the paper again. The nurse held the pad while I scribbled.

By the time I finished, he was already out the door, underlings in tow, leaving Nurse Claudia to answer the question I'd written: *WHY ARE MY HANDS TIED DOWN?*

And something strange: After watching the band of physicians depart, I looked at Claudia for an explanation of the big one's discourtesy. I caught her staring after them. Her lower lip trembled and a single tear slipped out of the corner of her eye onto her flushed cheek.

BOBBY

That morning, personnel from every branch of the medical industrial complex were lined up outside my room, all waiting for a crack at me. Med techs came from the lab with needles for every artery and vein in my wrinkled body, until I felt like a bloodless beige prune. Respiratory therapists administered elaborate breathing tests to determine what I told them the minute the wretched tube came out of my throat: I don't need the goddamn breathing machine! My first words! Dietitians, physical therapists, a different nurse every shift attending my every need. It was delightful. All that attention. And with the tube gone, I was able to visit with every one of them. All these smart youngsters were working so hard to find out what happened to my poor noggin.

Dear Bobby! He looked . . . Well, I was sorry to see that he'd gained weight, and his face was puffy. Probably the stress of having Mum conk out on him. That and eating fast food instead of my soups and salads, and also nobody around to tell him to shut down the computer games and go for a walk in the real world. He brought me lovely flowers from the grocery store, probably because he felt bad about not being there the first time I woke up.

"Don't worry, Mum," he said. "You're going to be just fine."

I read him like the label of one of his Red Stripes. He wasn't quite sure if I was going to be just fine, and neither was I.

"Who was that hideous doctor? Stegman? Is he a neurologist?"

"He's a neurosurgeon, Mum. Cut and cure. You whacked your head good, bruised one of your brain lobes or something, but when they scanned you, they spotted another scar or lesion in there. Could be nothing. They aren't worried about it yet. They say they just have to watch it and see if it grows. If it is something, he's the man to take it out."

"If he touches me I'll sue him for assault and battery. He's got the aura and astral body of Mussolini. Which reminds me, where's my bag? I need my crystals. I don't like going unprotected in the presence of such a malignant life force."

"Mum, he's a brilliant surgeon."

"We have surgeons in Maine. And if he's brilliant, find me a dull one. Bobby, what in God's name am I doing in Boston?"

"Mum, it's all about the brain scanners. They have the high tech ones here."

"Brain imaging! On me? How exciting. Tell me all about it."

"Well, they got PET scans, some fancy new kind of MRI. There's another one called a SPECT scan. They can't decide which one to do on you. We don't have those at the Kingdom. They're gonna scan you every which way and do surgery if they have to, then get you back home."

"PET scans! Pictures of my own brain at work! I want copies."

I kept looking at my boy. He was the same; I was different. The trip abroad in the borderlands between here and hereafter had turned me into someone else. It's like the physicists say: We're just holograms of particles moving through a universe of other holograms. I felt the same way after two years studying the Rig Veda at the University of Delhi in India. (Those were the glory days, before the bondage of marriage and full-time employment.) When I came home in 1954, south central Maine was a foreign country. The Androscoggin Valley was the same, but I was different. I couldn't throw rice at weddings without wondering: Why do we throw rice at weddings? Why is there no number 13 on our elevators? What happens when we make the sign of the cross? What exactly *is* Halloween all about?

Travel had turned me into a foreigner in my native land. But my son was still very much at home and always would be, so I had to be careful.

"Bobby, did you see Madeline Kruger's body that night?"

Bobby frowned, and I could see a memory worrying its way through the dim recesses of his docile brain, something he'd heard and promptly discounted, because he's about as inquisitive as a hibernating bear.

"No, Mum. I didn't see her. It was one crisis after another that night. They lost a little girl in the ICU right about the time you went down. Terrible thing. Earlier in the day, the pediatric cardiologist, Dr. Egas, had done a routine procedure to dilate the girl's pulmonary valve — supposed to be a low complication rate — but later that night they found out he had punctured the little girl's heart with the balloon catheter while he was in there. They took her back to the cath lab and tried to save her, but she died on the table. Eight years old. They brought the mom back there to be with the body. She was hysterical. She grabbed a scalpel and sliced up Egas real good with it. Took four of us to pull her off him. Now the chief medical officer is looking into whether Egas had been packing his nose that day."

He sniffed his thumb for me and was about to explain.

"I know what it means, Bobby. I wasn't too old to enjoy the sixties. What kind of a compound idiot monster takes narcotics before operating on a child?"

"After the little girl died, then you hit your

47

head, and in the middle of all that, we had an earthquake. Ruptured pipes, cracks in the basement flooring."

Bobby shuddered, and I could see him think better of mentioning something else.

"What?"

"Nothing, Mum," he said too quickly.

"How's it go?" I said, straining my old brain to shake loose what little Shakespeare I had left. " 'The quality of nothing hath not such need to hide itself.' Something about the poor girl?"

He looked sideways, meaning yes.

"She . . ." He caught his breath and rubbed his jowls with the meat of his palms. "They put her body in the morgue, of course, because you know there's *got* to be an autopsy on that one. And the cracks down there in the floors and walls. That's the old hospital down there, Mum. The one that burned down in your day. They built right over it. And you know how the earthquakes make the vermin go mad. Well, the rats got at the bodies —"

"Oh, no, Bobby —"

"Don't go asking around about the Mrs. Kruger business. It's been hushed up. The family is Catholic, and the suicide stuff is taboo."

"Of course it was one crisis after another that night, Bobby. It was a full moon and Friday, December thirteenth, what the Algonquin tribes called the full cold moon. Did you see that crazy old man in the gown come up to the nurses' station? Mr. Hyde, as I live and breathe. Walk into any emergency room in America and see what happens on a full moon Friday the thirteenth. I'm surprised you didn't get a plague of locusts with the Androscoggin River running red and backwards. What about Mrs. Kruger's suicide note? Did you read it?"

Bobby shook his head and scowled. "I didn't see it, Mum, and the full moon, that's just lunacy." He took a breath to change the subject, but I wasn't about to let him.

"Bobby, I need to see that note. I have to know what Madeline wrote about me. You've got to find a way to get a copy."

"Mum, I can't do that."

"You always found a way into the cookie jar."

"Please, I can't go rummaging around in a patient chart looking for a suicide note."

"Was there an autopsy?"

"I don't know." Another sideways look.

"You don't know?"

He winced and started sweating; he has a glandular disorder that makes him perspire profusely when he's the least bit nervous.

"Mrs. Kruger's body was down in the morgue, too. The rats — there must be armies of them in those old walls. They had LuvKraft Pest Control in the next day, but the bodies, they —"

"What about the orderly, the fellow sitting outside her room, dozing when he was supposed to be watching her. Chairman? Charmin?"

"Angelo Charron, Mum. He was gonna get fired for coming in drunk one too many times, anyway. Then he's got a patient on suicide precautions, and she somehow gets her hands on an ice pick. He's long gone, Mum."

"Then what about the nurse? Lauren? Laura? What did she say?"

"Laurel Werling. She got caught turning in for overtime she didn't work. Termination offense."

I grabbed one of my notebooks and wrote down the names.

"And nobody said anything about the condition of Madeline's body?"

"Condition? Like you mean, hacked arteries and dead as a ditch spade?"

I was a breath away from telling him about the driver ants. But I couldn't.

"Bobby, something's happening to me. I saw things —"

"Mum, they said you had some kind of fit. Then you whopped your head good. You died, for the love of Mike. They had to resuscitate you. Now you've been out of it for three days. Don't worry about seeing things."

"We've got to get back to Kingdom Hospital, Bobby. Something's happening. I know it."

"Mum, they aren't going to let you out of here until they find out about those spots in your brain."

"Tell me more about the scanning machines, Bobby. What's that SPECT one do?"

NEUROLOGY

Nurse Claudia and I spent most of the day just visiting together; I was her only patient, and we enjoyed each other's company. She said that, working in the ICU, she usually had two very sick patients to look after, so it was practically a holiday to have just a chatterbox like me, with no tubes or IVs to tend to. I learned that she had three young children and a husband who'd lost his computer programming job after the technology boom went bust. She had been working double shifts lately for the overtime, which meant that she'd been looking after me for sixteen hours a day since I'd whacked my head, even though half the time I wasn't quite all there. She was kind to Bobby, too, and explained all the procedures and equipment to us.

When I wasn't having a heart-to-heart with Claudia, I was scribbling frantically in my notebooks, trying to set down a true and accurate account of my travels outside my body in the space between heaven and earth.

That evening the doctors gave the order, and I was released from the intensive care unit and moved out onto Boston General's neurology ward. An orderly came to transport me and my things, but Nurse Claudia sent him away and said that she wanted to take me to my new quarters herself — an extraordinary kindness from an ICU nurse, for which I was grateful.

My new room was semiprivate: room 959, bed 2. The privacy curtains were drawn around bed 1, so I was not able to meet my roommate.

Claudia wheeled me in and helped me arrange my things. She freshened the water in the vase of flowers, put my bag on the nightstand, and helped me select an appropriate healing crystal for the new environment.

Then she sat at my bedside and put her finger on her lips. *Shhh.*

I looked toward bed 1 and the drawn curtain.

"She can't hear us," Claudia whispered.

If I wasn't mistaken, Claudia's eyes reddened again and tears welled. My heart went out to her immediately.

"What's wrong, Claudia, dear?"

"You know my situation," she whispered. "I have a good job, here. If I lost this job and had to find another . . . if I missed even a paycheck or two, it would destroy my family. It's all a house of credit cards right now, and I'm just able to make the interest payments until my husband finds work."

"Oh, my dear, I'll pray that he does. But why would you lose your job? You're an excellent and very kind nurse."

She put her hand tenderly on mine.

"Thank you. I'm telling you this only because I like you so much, and I have to ask you not to reveal to anyone what I'm about to share with you."

A tear squeaked out onto her cheek. She

brushed it away and looked out toward the hallway, afraid someone might come in.

"Claudia, look in my eyes and see what you already know: I would never betray your confidence and trust."

"I know you wouldn't. I'm just saying it for my own peace of mind. You must not tell a soul, not even Bobby."

"Tell me," I said. "Your secret will be safe."

"It's not a secret. It's a warning and important advice. If you do end up needing surgery —"

"Knock, knock!" A cheery male voice came from somewhere on the other side of my neighbor's drawn curtain. If the inhabitant of bed 1 had been sleeping, she'd have to be awake now.

Claudia stood up quickly and began straightening my things on the nightstand and tray table. She grabbed my Merlin crystal and held it up by its silk string.

"This one really is quite lovely," she said, as if she had just been admiring it and discussing it with me.

A man peeked around the privacy curtain and smiled at us. I recognized the comb-over and the subdominant stature of Dr. Metzger, the butcher/psychiatrist. He'd changed out of his white lab coat into a folksy tweed sport coat and black turtleneck. If he grew a beard and put on some elbow patches, he could fit right into the psychology department at Faust College.

"I can come back later, if you'd like?" he offered.

"Oh no, Dr. Metzger, that's all right," Claudia said. "I'm just getting my friend, Mrs. Druse, all settled into her new home."

She winked at me and added, "Sally, I'll be back day after tomorrow to finish our conversation."

"Look at you!" Dr. Metzger said to me. "Up and about, and riding the fence line already. I sensed that you weren't the type to stay bed-ridden for long."

"Well then, you have a good sense about people, which is how you wound up in psychiatry," I said.

"And how are you feeling? Any headaches? Dizziness? Your cranial checks were shipshape, and the lab work shows all values in normal range." He made a thumbs-up at me, as if I were the Little Leaguer and he my coach.

"I have headaches, but otherwise I feel fine. I'd love to get the pictures of my brain done and then go home to Lewiston. Dr. Massingale can watch over me there and look after my headaches."

As he talked, he made his way over to the chair vacated by Claudia.

"Well, yes," he said, "Dr. Massingale referred you to our service and asked us to do some brain imaging, but she also asked us to look at the total you as well, Mrs. Druse. How were you feeling before all of this happened? Any unusual sensations or episodes? Any strange feelings, emotions, unusual thought patterns?"

He took a seat, opened a chart, and looked to be settling in for a nice long psychiatric examination, for which I would undoubtedly be charged a handsome fee. Furthermore, it seemed the diagnostic session was to take place within earshot of another patient I hadn't met yet.

"Excuse me," I said, and turned in the direction of the bed next to me. "Hello?" I said into the drawn curtain. "Knock, knock. I'm told I have a roommate. Is that true?"

Dr. Metzger smiled and stopped me with a gentle there-there wave of his hand. "Mrs. Druse, really there's no reason to be concerned about disturbing your neighbor. She's . . . unresponsive right now."

"In a coma?" I asked.

"Not exactly," he said. "She can't hear what we are saying. Correction — she can't *process* what we are saying."

"Does *she* have a name?"

"Yes. Nancy Conlan has been here for, oh, several months. She won't —" His hand just fluttered off in the direction of the land where nothing matters.

I lowered my voice anyway. "I don't need a psychiatrist, Doctor." I was polite, even pleasant, about it — no need to get nasty. Yet.

"No, probably not," he admitted, "but we'd like to rule out as many things as possible while you're with us here in Boston. We'd like to do another scan or two and some tests to see, well, to see what's going on with you."

He didn't elaborate. *What's going on with me?*

"What do the scans show? Exactly," I asked. "Is it possible to look at the scans and see my highly developed capacity for mystical experiences?"

He almost laughed, but he caught himself in time. A flatlander, I could tell; probably didn't believe or care about the spiritual life — his or anybody else's.

"The scans are so expensive, we're still using them only to diagnose and treat life-threatening illnesses, at least here in this hospital."

I didn't know him well enough to be blunt, but tumors or no, my seventy-five-year-old skull was going to the grave unopened, of that I was sure. I had no intention of having surgery, certainly not under the likes of Dr. Stegman. All I wanted from Metzger were a few of the more interesting brain scans and EEGs, which he could order up with a stroke of his Montblanc pen.

"I appreciate the value of the brain imaging," I said. "Did you see in *The New York Times* where the Dalai Lama is also passionately interested in it?"

"I . . . missed that."

"He is, and he's made several visits to America to meet with neuroscientists who are scanning and studying the brains of Zen monks while they are meditating."

"Interesting," he said. "You'll be getting an MRI scan this afternoon. So you and the Dalai Lama can compare notes."

"Delightful. I assure you, Doctor, if you study my scans carefully you will notice an exceptional amount of activity in the brain centers associated with positive emotions, especially compassion, mindfulness, and spirituality."

He at least feigned interest at this point.

"Yes, I'm sure we will see evidence of your . . . *spiritedness*, Mrs. Druse. I'd like to ask you about some of your mystical experiences. Dr. Massingale mentioned in your history that you have certain . . . gifts."

Mmm. Maybe not a complete flatlander after all, if he was curious about gifts.

"How shall I say this? I am unusually sensitive to the world of the spirits, to wonder, and to the unity of all beings and things. Nondual awareness, some call it. Are you familiar with James Austin's *Zen and the Brain*?"

"I'm not. Perhaps I should be," said Metzger. "You meditate, yes?"

"Every day. And I pray, too."

"I ask you about peculiar sensations or visual disturbances because it is not at all uncommon for patients to experience auras and seizure activity without even realizing it. Subjectively the patient experiences the seizure as a daydream or perhaps a mystical experience. A vision of some kind? Voices? Have you ever sensed an unseen presence? Or perhaps heard a voice?"

I smiled and kept my counsel, made it look as if I was hard at work searching my memory. These institutional medical scientists can be ruthless if you confide the intimate details of your spiritual life. To them, imagination, religious devotion, and mystical awareness are all symptoms of mental illness.

"No visions that I can think of," I said. "Just the mindfulness that comes with meditation. No voices that I can think of. But I know where you're headed. That's the old Thomas Szasz quote, right? 'If you talk to God, you are praying; if God talks to you, you have schizophrenia.' Is that your line of inquiry here?"

I don't think Metzger was ready for a batty septuagenarian to be quoting renowned psychiatrists back at him.

"Oh, yes, Szasz. That's a good one. I've heard that," he said. "The reason we ask so many questions about auras and potential seizures is that they can be very harmful to the brain," he explained. "They may feel either unpleasant or frightening or pleasant and transcendent to the patient, but they are actually electrical discharges. Neurons firing, and those cells aren't meant to discharge electricity in continuous bursts, like flushing a toilet over and over. Eventually the cells wear out, much the same way a battery dies. But unlike batteries, brain cells can't be replaced."

"Dead brain cells would be a tragedy," I said. "Especially for a young person."

I watched him ponder that one. Was I saying that it *wouldn't* be a tragedy for an old person?

"I'm not fond of medications, Dr. Metzger.

So if this is all leading up to me taking some kind of medicine, I don't think that will be happening."

My preemptive strike on the subject of medication disconcerted him, and I saw him prepare for a counterstrike, so I jumped on ahead to appeasement of sorts.

"Perhaps the brain images will convince me that I need to take medications. I assume they'll tell us something about that, yes? Otherwise we wouldn't be doing them?"

"The scans will tell us more about the fresh hemorrhage you suffered in your fall, and may also help us get a better view of that older-looking lesion or scar in the frontal lobe. Which reminds me —"

He riffled through his papers and pulled out a report and refreshed his memory.

"Yes. When the radiologist looked at the images of that frontal lobe spot, the older scar, he thought it looked almost like it was inflicted transorbitally."

I looked at him and waited for an explanation.

He put his index finger just above his left eyelid and just under his eyebrow.

"Through the eye socket," he said. "Up here? Any childhood head trauma? Any falls onto sharp objects? Anybody poke you in the eye or above the eye with a stick or a pen, perhaps? Anything like that?"

I shook my head. "I'm quite certain I'd remember that," I said.

"I'm sure you would," he said. "You may have had a seizure that night when you were visiting your friend at Kingdom Hospital, which in turn caused you to fall and whack your poor head. That's why I asked you if you recall anything strange or unusual associated with that episode. Any visual or auditory disturbances? Any peculiar sensations or experiences?"

I put on my best happy face and made my eyes nice and sparkly for the good doctor.

"Well, I have another Thomas Szasz quote you might like," I offered.

"Edify me, Mrs. Druse, please."

" 'In the animal kingdom, the rule is, eat or be eaten; in the human kingdom, define or be defined.' You aren't trying to define me, are you, Dr. Metzger?"

CHOSEN

I must have slipped into one of my little cat-naps, because the next time I opened my eyes, there was Bobby in the chair next to my bed, his curly unkempt head buried in the sports section of *The Boston Globe*.

"Bobby, I'm so glad you're here. What did you find out back in Lewiston?"

He leaned over and kissed me on the fore-head, but then he sank back into his chair and withdrew again into his newspaper.

"Find out about what, Mum?" he mumbled.

"What did you find out about Madeline Kruger? Did you find a copy of her suicide note?"

He groaned behind the paper.

"Mum, they told me the only way to get it is to contact the family. The charts are all locked up in medical records. They said the note might not be with her chart anyway. They said the police or the coroner might have it. You don't want me to call the police or the coroner, do you?"

"Who's going through her effects, Bobby? She's got two daughters and a son. They're all grown up now. Responsible adults, I hope! Somebody's got to be taking care of what she left in the house. I want you to call them and tell them that I was with their mother during the last hours of her life, because the hospital called me and said that Madeline had addressed certain comments to me. The last words she wrote in this world, Bobby, were to me. Do you understand?"

A big sigh, and he hitched the paper up even higher, because he didn't want me to catch him looking at the latest line on sports betting. He knows I hate it when he throws good money away on the Red Sox and the Celtics.

"Mum, I'll try. Maybe I can stop by their old house. I used to have a cold frosty or two with Ray Kruger when he hung out at the Piece of Work and the Holly. He was living in Reno, but he's back now. The old lady — er, I mean, his

61

mum must have left him a little dough, because I heard he was in the back room of the Piece the other night looking for a game of nine-ball and some action."

"Bobby, I need that note. I have a sense that all of these things are related somehow. I don't know why. Also," I said, indicating my first notebook, which was already almost full, "I need another notebook, a nice fat one."

"Yeah, you've been writing a lot. Is it all about the spirits?"

"Bobby, I can feel it. I'm being chosen for something."

"Chosen for what, Mum?" he mumbled from behind the paper.

I decided it was time to let him in on at least some of my secrets.

"I am being singled out to see things that other people can't or won't see," I said.

"Well, you've always wanted to see things, haven't you, Mum?"

"Wanted to, yes, Bobby, but now it's actually *happening.* I've seen — I think I've been chosen to receive revelations. The way Swedenborg was allowed to travel through heaven and hell and interview angels."

"Oh, no, not the Sweden-bozo again," he groaned. "Mum, if it's not the Dalai Lama, it's this Swedenborg guy. You can read that stuff all you want. You know I don't mind. I've even schlepped to the used book stores and the libraries to find those out-of-print books for you, but when you talk that stuff to other people, they think you're daffy."

"I haven't told you, Bobby, but I'm having visions."

"Visions, Mum? Like into the future? Are you feeling like you have special powers? Second sight and whatnot? Can you tell me, are the Celts gonna spank the Knicks tomorrow night in the Garden? Can you tell me if that nurse named Carrie Von Trier who works nights on the pediatric ward back at the Kingdom has a boyfriend?"

"Bobby, I've traveled in the borderlands between life and death."

"Mum, the one psychiatrist already thinks you're crackers. If you don't stop going on about visions, they'll lock you up in a quiet room on the psych ward and keep you here for a month. And you won't get to take your bag of magic tricks in with you, Mum. They'll be afraid of you hanging yourself with a pendulum string or cutting yourself with a crystal.

"You don't want to be locked up there with those Osama Been Looney Toons, do you?"

BED 1

The next morning, two young nurses — Jennifer and Tiffany — wheeled in a utility cart stacked with towels and bathing supplies. With illness and death crawling like yellow fog along

63

the walls in this medical megalopolis, these two pretty young things in April bloom seemed garishly vigorous. Maybe one of them would be able to put up with Bobby if he lost some weight and quit smoking that pipe? They asked me if I was comfortable, if I had everything I needed, if I'd seen my doctor and so on.

"Yes, yes, I'm fine," I said. "I was just getting up to meet my roommate."

They looked at each other, then back at me.

"Well, we're going to give Nancy her bath right now," said Jennifer. "Maybe you should wait."

A single violent rattle sounded from behind the curtain, as if the patient had struck or shaken the bedrail.

"Oh," I said, "then she's awake?"

They looked at each other again.

"She's awake, but, uh, she needs her privacy," said Tiffany. Then she forced a big smile. "Dr. Stegman gave you ambulatory privileges. Perhaps you'd like to walk around a little? Stretch your legs?"

"The day I need his permission to walk —" I said.

I had to admit that a stroll sounded enjoyable. So I put on my robe and my Merlin crystal and shuffled out for some exploring.

As I was preparing to go, I heard the two nurses behind the curtain washing and chatting.

"Stay on this floor, Mrs. Druse," one of the girls called.

"Yes," said the other, "or we'll come and hunt you down."

They seemed to be having a merry old time, so I left them to their work and ventured out into the wide world of Boston General.

Dr. Metzger's little session yesterday troubled me, I suppose, because I had to consider that he might be right. To my knowledge I'd never had a seizure of any kind, nor had my neurologist at Kingdom Hospital, Dr. Massingale, ever proposed that as a diagnosis to me. Of course I knew that seizures come in many different forms, not just the familiar grand mal, where the epileptic falls down frothing at the mouth. I guessed that the doctors here were wondering if I might be having petit mals, small seizures, difficult to detect on clinical examination.

I had no doubt that if I had confided in Metzger and shared the details of my near-death experience, he would have defined me as an epileptic in the grip of seizures. My head hurt and the sore parts of me were ready to believe in anything that might explain what had happened to me that December night at Kingdom Hospital. All my life I had waited for an angel, a vision, a journey out of myself, a visitation so bracing that I would gasp with delight at a world full of wonders and see with my new eyes naked what my faith had told me for decades: that the spiritual realm, though invisible, is inseparable from the material world, and that life circulates like blood through them both. No here. No hereafter. Only a great unity! And Sally Druse right there in the thick of it!

What if these seizures could explain all the extraordinary things that I had ever experienced? Not only Madeline's infested corpse, but the transcendence and prayerful joy that was mine in the deep reveries of meditation? What then? What if the vast inscape of my entire spiritual life derived from a lesion?

Patients and staff streamed by me in the busy hallways of Boston General. Sick and well. Busy and indolent. I looked into the eyes of everyone who walked by me, wondering what aberrations of brain chemistry and organic syndromes made them who they were. Did that awful surgeon Stegman have a pomposity lesion somewhere in there? And if so, would he agree to go under the knife to have it removed and have his personality repaired? Did neurosurgeons propose cutting into Barbra Streisand's or Rush Limbaugh's head because of the crazy shit they say?

When I returned from my jaunt, the room was quiet, and I resolved then and there to meet my mysterious roommate, who apparently was so ill that she could neither hear nor respond to my voice, and who needed two nurses to bathe her.

I sat on the edge of my bed and faced the curtain between us. The morning sunrise slanted in through the windows and made the flowers Bobby had brought me even lovelier in the new light.

"Mrs. Conlan? My name is Sally Druse. I'm

your new roommate and I'd like to come over and see you, if it's a convenient time."

Nobody answered, even though, after half a minute or so, I heard a soft groan, followed by gurgling, then metal rattling again, as if Mrs. Conlan had grabbed the bedrail and shaken it hard.

I'm the neighborly sort, so I got out of my bed and went to the foot of hers, where I could see an opening in the draperies. The linen curtain made a pale scrim and diffused the harsh light of the sun into a nimbus that lit the interior with an otherworldly light.

On the bed a gaunt, ghastly human figure lay supine, with pillows wedged here and there on either side of her, without which I had the impression she would shrivel into a sideways fetal position and perish. She appeared youthful — thirty or so — but with a lifetime's worth of suffering etched into the lineaments of her grimacing face. Her neck was extended and arched, almost as if she were trying to see something above the head of her bed. She appeared wide awake, but her eyeballs had rolled back into her hollow, dark sockets, where gravity alone controlled their listless movements. Likewise her mouth had fallen open and seemed permanently ajar, her chin shuddering with each breath. Her hands were curled up in front of her like the talons of a dead bird, with splints fastened at each wrist, to keep the fingers from curling into themselves. As I watched, she began

67

working her mouth as if she were chewing without ever swallowing. She was appallingly thin, a human leftover from nature's repast, her miserable figure lit by a morning radiance that was too harsh for my ancient eyes and my tender heart.

I spotted the source of the rattling: Her hands were tethered to the steel bedrails, and every so often, her arms jerked spastically and yanked the railings against the bed frame.

"My poor Mrs. Conlan." I spoke aloud, but words were of no use.

A tap on the door. It was an orderly pushing a wheelchair, and right behind him, son Bobby.

"C'mon, Mum," said Bobby. "We're going upstairs to take some pictures of that crackpot brain of yours."

THE BRAIN OF E. DRUSE

More brain scans! How exciting. I didn't have the heart to tell Dr. Metzger that I wasn't going to let the likes of Dr. Stegman poke around inside my brain, no matter what showed up on my scans. (There's a little legal theory I know a lot about called informed consent.) But I saw no harm in indulging our mutual curiosity about what big doings were happening between the walls of my skull.

Bobby and the orderly wheeled me to a separate wing that must have been devoted exclusively to the domain of the brain. All the signs on the wall began with *neuro* — neuropharmacology, neuropsychology, neurophysiology.

Finally, at the end of a windowless corridor, we came to a large door with a huge handle on it that looked like a closed bank vault. The technician, a nice young man named Michael Baxley (from Portland, Maine!), came out and informed me about the extremely powerful magnetic fields to which I would soon be exposed and questioned me closely about any metal components I may have acquired in life's journey — prostheses, pacemakers, orthopedic screws, shrapnel.

"Did you know that the Dalai Lama is intensely interested in brain imaging?" I asked him. "He's in cahoots with several Western neuroscientists who are imaging the brains of Buddhist monks to measure what occurs in the brain during meditation and mindfulness."

"You don't say," said Michael Baxley. "Nobody's ever told me that before."

"Mum, lay off with the Dalai Lama, would you?" said Bobby.

My interest in the Dalai Lama embarrassed Bobby, I guessed. But why? I don't get embarrassed when he's interested in beer and the Red Sox, or when he plays that damn old ABBA album all day long.

By the time I got into the scanning chamber I was beaming with anticipation. I assumed my health insurance would cover most of it, but it occurred to me that I might be able to charge these neuroresearchers for a look inside the brain of Eleanor Druse. I'd show them a scan image for the record books if I could work myself into one of my meditations or deep prayer states before they took their pictures.

Once in the scanning room, I felt as if the technicians were preparing to launch me into space via an alien abduction tube. I had to lie very still while the MRI was working, they said. I would be able to hear them and speak to them, and they would be able to tell me when I had to hold still and when I could take a break and wriggle around to get the blood flowing and keep my old limbs from falling asleep.

They slid me deep inside a huge cylindrical scanner. I had the sensation that my little cranium had been nestled in some vast cosmological turbine.

On the inside panel of the beige doughnut, at eye level, I saw a tiny metal tag embossed with letters and numbers, a code or serial number, a long meaningless alphanumeric sequence.

"Okay, Mrs. Druse," said Michael, "we're going to start the machine now. We aren't taking scans yet, just warming her up, okay?"

"Fire away!" I said.

I began my meditation in earnest, trying to slip as quickly as possible into the strong but gentle stream of being that flows just below consciousness.

"Mrs. Druse, the machine is all ready, and

now comes the very important part about holding absolutely still. Can you do that for us?"

"I won't budge a jiggedy jot!"

I stared straight ahead at the letters and numbers, which became ciphers glowing with a celestial light. I didn't so much as blink and yet they changed right before my eyes into occult symbols or cryptograms, iridescent and changeable, as if the data from the device was flashing by on a digital readout for me to see.

I closed my eyes and felt myself disappear inside the material universe. I have practiced yoga and meditation for most of my adult life, and I have struggled along the steep path that leads to mystical self-transcendence. Finally it happened, right there in the scanner: my first truly extraordinary state of consciousness. The boundary between me and the rest of the universe dissolved. I was no longer myself seeing matter, I was matter seeing myself. The polyurethane shell surrounding me was still beige and textured, but it was also perfect, profound, and meant to be. Like me, it was part of eternity. I didn't have to do or say, be or think. I was. I was Brahman, the single absolute being animating and sustaining the entire universe, and every time I breathed, I exhaled a new universe.

Outside, Michael Baxley was shaving my noodle into sheets of transparent color, like stained glass, to be studied by computer networks, but here inside, I was exhaling one gorgeous infinite universe after another.

71

I could hardly wait to tell Bobby all about it, and I was careful not to move and spoil the photos they were taking of my big event.

THE NOTE

Bobby is not the toughest page to read in the book of humanity. When he came in my room and took a seat near my bed without bringing the newspaper with him, I knew something was up.

Words weren't necessary. I looked at him; he looked away. Then he reached inside his coat and pulled out two sheets of paper he'd stuffed into his pocket.

"I had a beer with Ray Kruger."

"Good boy, Bobby. You got Madeline's suicide note, then?"

Outright success has never been in his repertoire. He squirmed and looked away again.

"Ray says his big sis, Hilda, is the executor of his mum's estate. When Ray asked about any notes his mum left, Hilda got pissy and said their mum was a writer, and she was always writing crazy stuff, horror stories and whatnot, including stories about characters who wrote notes and killed themselves."

"I see. Then ask Hilda if we can read her mum's last tale about a character named Madeline who wrote a note about a person named Sally Druse and then killed herself."

"Mum, they're Catholics. You can't talk suicide to them because it's like telling them their mum is in hell. Plus, Ray said he would never let anybody see the whole note. He said it's too disturbing. His mum was a walking psychodrama when she wrote it."

"I'm not saying she killed herself or is in hell or is a walking psychodrama. I just want to see what she wrote to me in the note."

Bobby smiled. "My argument exactly, Mum. I asked him for the parts about you. Ray's sister let him see the note, and he tried to copy down the parts about you when she wasn't looking. He says he can't be sure he got it all, but he tried. He also says you can't tell anybody, or Hilda will cut him out of the will money."

"Good boy, Bobby. I won't tell a soul. Read it to me while I hunt for my glasses."

"Let's see, here," Bobby mumbled. "He's right about one thing, Mum. It's three-headed weird. Flowery, too. I'd leave it all alone. She's missing a few buttons on her remote if you ask me. Okay, she says:

"God has blessed Sally Druse with a memory more merciful than mine. I will not disturb her peace with cruel remembrance. We were children when Evil touched us, but our childhoods go back thousands of years, farther than the memory of man. Sally forgot her scars. My wounds still fester. I have asked God for forgiveness and forgetfulness, but my prayers go unanswered. I leave this

73

life confident that I have seen the worst of Evil here among the living. I can only improve my lot by rushing into the secret house of death."

By the time Bobby had finished reading, I'd found my glasses and was trembling all over. I felt the same coldness swelling inside me that I'd felt the night Madeline tried to take her own life. Some dreadful nameless memory walled off from the rest of me tried to erupt into consciousness. Even though it was inside of me, I felt outside of it and trying to break in, as if I were feeling my way along a black wall in the dead of night, searching for an opening of some kind so that I could discover what was on the other side.

My hands were shaking when Bobby handed me the paper, and I read it over carefully. *Sally's memory more merciful than mine . . . We were children when Evil touched us . . .*

Again the terrible sensation that a memory was just out of reach, but there on the threshold of remembering, I paused and wondered if I should stop probing blindly in the darkness, because what if I disturbed some ghastly thing better left alone?

Bobby still had the second paper in his hand.

"What's that one, Bobby?"

"This one Ray gave me outright, because she wrote it to you the very night she died. After she woke up in the hospital and started talking nonsense about you, they asked her did she want them to give you a message, and she wrote you this note. Nobody knows what it means. She must have been gaga on the pills. That's when I called you from the hospital."

Bobby handed me a sheet of Kingdom Hospital letterhead stationery of the sort they keep in drawers at the bedside. Scrawled in large letters with ugly jagged downstrokes and lightning bolts for cross strokes were the words:

DEAR SALLY: THE LITTLE GIRL WHO SAVED US IS STILL LOST. SHE IS BACK AMONG THE LAIR OF THE LIVING. THE FIRE DID NOT KILL HER. SHE NEEDS OUR HELP. COME SEE ME.

At the bottom of the page, she'd signed it in what looked like a schoolgirl's hand: MADDY KRUGER, November 2nd, 1939.

Again, the queasy sensation that I was on the verge of coming into a clearing in memory's dark forest, but I didn't know what I would find there. A witch? A goblin? A shallow mass grave?

"In case of fire, break glass," I said.

Bobby stared at me and frowned. He looked like a Jersey bull chewing a pinch of Red Man instead of his cud.

"What are you saying, Mum?"

"I don't know," I said. "I don't know why I said that. I thought it the other night."

75

He rolled his eyes and looked back at me, as if he was waiting for me to grow another head.

"Bobby, what does it mean? 'The little girl who saved us?' What can it mean?"

"It means Mrs. Kruger was section eight, Mum. Certifiable. Squirrel food."

"The fire did not kill her? What fire, Bobby? What little girl saved us? Why can't I remember? It's Alzheimer's, I know it. If I get that, just go on and feed my bones to Skipper, will you promise me that?"

"Says November 1939," he grunted, "and she's talking about a fire. When did the old Kingdom Hospital burn down, Mum? Around then, wasn't it? Hell, I could look at the cornerstone on the new one when I go back to work on Monday."

"I was in that old hospital," I said, "right before it burned. With Madeline, in fact. We had whooping cough. But I can't remember it, Bobby. I've never been able to remember it. They say high fevers and such will do that to you. Just kind of wipes out the old data banks."

The little girl who saved us is still lost?

THE FAMILY

That evening Nancy Conlan's husband, Dave, came for a visit and brought his mother with him for reinforcement. They showed up just after the dinner hour with fresh flowers, a com-

76

forter, more cards and letters to arrange on Nancy's tray table, and another snapshot to add to the collection of photographs on her nightstand — all of them featuring Nancy with her three kids.

Dave Conlan had rolling shoulders and bulging arm muscles and was hunched in a perpetual half crouch, as if he'd spent most of his life lifting and hauling. He had an old-style flattop and empty eyes that shone a steady, unblinking blue, like panel lights indicating their owner was on autopilot — probably had been since around the time his wife didn't wake up from routine surgery to remove an arachnoid cyst near her brain stem.

Dave's mother, Virginia, was in her fifties and wore a black beautician's smock and an ID badge that said HELENA'S HAIR HOUSE in pink with a matching pink hairdo logo and pink scissors. She had sculptured nails that were too long and too red and the overtinted, overdone 'do of somebody in the beauty salon business.

She showed me a photo of Nancy and the three kids gathered around a picnic table somewhere in the irretrievable past, a golden retriever frolicking in the mix of little kid legs. The three children were waving bubble wands, and several well-wrought specimens drifted overhead. Nancy's smile was incandescent, her eyes laughing, as she stretched out her hand, the summer sun shining in her lustrous hair, her slender fingers reaching out to touch a big wobbly one with rainbows swirling all over its skin, a fleeting diaphanous thing of intense beauty floating just out of reach.

It's why God gave man the genius to invent photography: So there could be tangible proof that happiness is more than something we remember; it actually happens sometimes.

When I shook Dave's huge calloused hand, it was like sliding my fingers into a catcher's mitt. I shuddered to think of those three small children at home, and wages earned by the labor of those big rough hands going to sustain the barely breathing husk tied to the bed, a pathetic memorial to some horrible catastrophe.

Virginia added the photo to the bedside collection, and an awkward moment intervened, because I could tell she wanted to draw the privacy curtain in case she had to sit down for the not uncommon good long cry. But she caught my eye and thought it might be rude to shut me out, I suppose, so she left the curtain open. A situation I could not improve by inviting her to close it if she wished.

She and Dave lined up on either side of Nancy and watched her breathe for a minute or two. Then Virginia brushed Nancy's hair and complained about how the poor girl's complexion was getting even paler, and how it was all because they couldn't take her outside in the wheelchair anymore, because she was stiff as lumber, and because of that feeding tube sewn into her stomach.

"She's getting that white stuff in her mouth," Virginia said to Dave. "Look there," she continued. "Remind me to ask the nurse about that medicine we used to swab in her mouth. There, Nan, that's okay. Davy's here."

After that, Nancy's parents showed up, Renn and Margie. Margie was a squat, round, feeble, and tentative woman in a peasant skirt with a polyester sweatshirt that read "Falmouth on Old Cape Cod" and red hair pulled back and rubber-banded in a haphazard fashion. Renn was a florid, portly gent in a tight red rayon bowling shirt that barely covered his prodigious belly. Over the left pocket of his shirt was written RENN, and across the shoulders in back RENN'S RAIDERS.

"Our little girl waking up yet?" asked Renn.

Nobody answered him, and nobody took offense. I sensed it was just something he said whenever he came here, and would always say as long as they kept what had been his little girl alive.

Nurse Tiffany came in and removed a thermometer from Nancy's armpit.

"How's she doing?" asked Renn.

"Her blood pressure is back to normal," said Tiffany. "No fever. Her electrolytes are better with the new tube feedings. She's putting out more urine, and that's good."

"Her sores better?" asked Virginia.

"They debrided her sores today. The dermatologist says there's improvement."

79

"They do any more tests on her brain?"

"I don't think so," said Tiffany. "I don't think any were ordered."

"Well, somebody said something way back in the beginning about maybe going back in there and seeing if they could fix things," said Renn. "There any more talk of that?"

I could see Virginia take a big here-we-go-again breath; Dave just stared at Nancy with those autopilot blues.

"That's something you should talk to the doctors about, I think," said Tiffany smoothly, "maybe one of the neurologists? Dr. Cantrell or Dr. Mayfield?" Then she slipped into a playful, scolding tone. "Have you been keeping that list of questions for the doctor I told you to make? So you'll remember your questions when you see them?"

"Aw," Renn said and shuffled his feet, and I could see him blushing in the radiance of Tiffany's effortless vitality, her good looks, her absolute self-confidence when it came to handling painful inquiries about death and terminal illness. Despite her tender years, these grim affairs were already routine for her. Brain damage was as familiar to her as a run in her stocking or spoiled fruit.

"Has he been keeping his list?" she asked Margie in a just barely chiding tone.

Margie shook her head. "He talks. Eats. Drinks. That's about it. Bowls on Thursday nights."

"She t'ain't woke up, even once?" Renn asked Tiffany.

"Well," said Tiffany, "she wakes up. But I haven't seen her respond to anyone yet." She tilted her head and lifted her shaped eyebrows. "I'm sorry."

"See?" Renn said to Margie. "She wakes up. That's not the problem. So there's some hope then," he added.

Margie started in a quiet cry.

Virginia reached out and took Dave's hand.

Tiffany started out the door, but Renn called after her.

"Tell the doctors I want to talk to them, then. And I'll make a list. Okay?"

"Yes, sir," said Tiffany. "I'll tell them."

THE CHANNELING CRYSTAL

I tried to give the family privacy, even though the curtain was half open. I rummaged in my bag to find my channeling crystal. When I have a problem I can't solve by using my deteriorating powers of reason, I reach for a good channeling crystal and use it to prospect for knowledge deep inside myself, calling upon resources within me but beyond my reasoning.

A good pendulum provides a link to the subconscious, the Jungian unconscious, and all the other unmapped realms of the interior, which operate outside the feeble flashlight beam of

81

mere consciousness. When one asks a question of the pendulum, the answer comes from one's own inner vibrations. I held the crystal in my hand, touched the termination points with my index fingers and thumbs, and closed my eyes. I let the voices of Nancy's family come and go, along with any images. I asked for guidance and listened.

"What you got there, lady?" asked Renn.

I opened my eyes and introduced myself to Renn and Margie.

"What's that you're holding there, ma'am?" he asked. "If you don't mind me prying."

I showed him my channeling crystal.

"Look at that," said Renn and motioned for Virginia and Dave to come have a look. "What's it do for you?"

"Oh, it helps me focus my mental energies. If I close my eyes and meditate while I'm holding it, it helps channel energy from my unconscious."

"Wow," said Renn. "Lookie there, it makes rainbows on the walls."

"Can you see into the future with it?" asked Virginia.

"Only in bad movies," I said. "If you have the proper crystal on a string and use it as a pendulum, you can sometimes receive guidance, but the information comes from within. Not from the future or from the spirits."

"Hey," said Renn. "I got to get out of here to my bowling game. Do you think that next time

I come around, you could ask it some things for me?"

"I'd be happy to," I said.

STEGMAN

I was on needles and pins (or noodles and prunes, as my mother used to say) waiting for my official meeting with the doctors about my scans. Not only had I achieved a mystical transformation, but it was also certifiable, because it had happened right there under the scanner. The doctors were late for our meeting, probably because they were still upstairs watching reruns of my enlightenment on the monitors, unable to tear themselves away from the big event. Maybe my scans could inspire them to start a whole new study here at Boston General on brain imaging and mystical states. Maybe my scans would appear in *Science* or *Nature*, right next to the scans of a Zen monk from Tibet experiencing nirvana.

It was all too exciting. I felt guilty being blessed with such good fortune while Nancy Conlan languished in the next bed. This morning she'd been grimacing, gagging, and lurching spastically, tugging at her restraints, and rattling the bedrails. When I had asked Claudia about the restraints in the ICU, she said nurses were required to use them to keep the patients from yanking out their tubes. Case in point: Nancy had pulled out her feeding tube twice.

Once that morning, while I was waiting for the doctors, Nancy laughed out loud, or at least it sounded like a laugh, which was eerie in the extreme. I got out of bed and went to have a look. She paralyzed me with a glance, because she seemed to be staring right through my eyes and out the back of my head. When she breathed, she made a soft rasping sound and the dark hole of her mouth got bigger and smaller. She grimaced, and her mouth started that gumming motion again, like she was chewing on a big nothing bone, using her lips instead of her teeth. Then her eyeballs rolled back in their sockets, and she was gone again.

It occurred to me that her brain might have a few flickering flames of consciousness left — just enough to realize that it was the feeding tube keeping her alive, and maybe she knew in her own way that it had to go. But the hospital administrators weren't about to let that happen, so they had tied her down in bed.

I asked Tiffany — or was it Jennifer? (I mixed them up daily) — to give Nancy something to calm her down before her family came to visit that evening. I died inside at the thought of her husband or her parents finding Nancy grimacing or laughing, or lunging spastically against her restraints.

I heard an angry voice, one I instantly recognized from my first waking moments in the intensive care unit.

"Good morning, madam," said Dr. Stegman. "And how are we feeling?"

For this excursion, the alpha male surgeon had brought a reduced entourage consisting only of his sycophantic manservant, Metzger, and three other doctors.

Stegman took a seat in Bobby's chair, and the others spread out along the low-lying heating and air-conditioning register, which doubled as a shelf for extra bedding and supplies. Stegman used his opposable thumbs to scroll his way through a handheld computer while Metzger introduced the two mature females, Dr. Cantrell and Dr. Mayfield, as neurologists, and another subdominant male, Dr. Gilmore, as a radiologist specializing in magnetic resonance imaging. I searched Dr. Gilmore's face for any lingering traces of astonishment left over from his study of my remarkable scan patterns; none in evidence. Instead, he gave me a perfunctory smile and began reviewing his notes and "presenting" to Stegman.

As soon as introductions were completed, Stegman put away his toy computer, shook his blown-dry mane at me, and said, "Madam, it's high time for us to come clean with each other."

I looked at the other doctors, but they looked down at their notes.

Stegman continued, "We now have indications from the electroencephalograms and the magnetic resonance imaging that strongly suggest you have a seizure disorder."

85

My hands trembled in my lap. I didn't want the beast to see my fear, so I clutched at my channeling crystal (I'd worn it because I knew Mussolini would be here).

"You have proof of seizures? I don't have seizures," I said uncertainly. "I don't . . . remember anything like that."

"I assure you that you have complex partial seizures. Probably often. And these seizures are most likely being caused either by the fresh hemorrhage in your temporal lobe or by the older-looking, more puzzling irregularity in your frontal lobe."

"There's been a mistake." My voice shook, even as I fought to control it. "I think I can explain. I deliberately worked myself into an intense spiritual experience while I was inside the scanning device. I meditated before and during the scan, because I was curious about what parts of my brain would be active during my meditation. I inadvertently had an episode of true enlightenment, ladies and gentlemen, and I fear that you mistook the energy from my mystical experience for the electrical discharges from a common seizure."

Stegman leaned forward and peered at me as if he were an eminent entomologist and I a rare species of bug mounted and wriggling on a pin. He uttered the most fearsome and deadly assessment in the physician's repertory, a declaration that should excite terror in the hearts of all patients who hear it used to describe their diseases or disorders: "Interesting." On a medical doctor's lips, the adjective portends months if not years of testing, pain, suffering, and debilitation, while the medical industrial complex brings its technological and diagnostic might to bear on the fascinating intricacies of an ill-defined infirmity. No expense will be spared to understand and explain the *interesting* disorder, until its mystery is defined . . . even if, as is often the case, it's done on autopsy after the patient has died. "Very interesting" can be even worse. The ancient Chinese curse — *May you live in interesting times* — could be modified for moderns to read: *May you develop interesting diseases.*

"Madam, I gather Dr. Metzger was ever so gentle with you the other day in suggesting to you that you may have a seizure disorder. My psychiatric colleagues tend to be big-hearted camp counselors worried about damaging the patient's fragile self-esteem, so they do a kind of ignoramus waltz around the issue of seizures. He asked you about your symptoms, and you were not forthcoming."

"I told him what I thought he needed to know," I said. "And I didn't tell him what was none of his business."

"We've all had decades of experience dealing with this kind of thing," said Stegman. "You have what is called a temporal lobe personality." Nods all around again. "And since you are so coy with us and insist on keeping your symptoms to yourself, I shall tell you a little bit about what is going on with you."

He appeared to be making notes about something else, perhaps another patient, while he rattled off the tiresome details of my condition.

"Lately, you've had extreme sensations, hallucinations, which may take the form of strange odors, sights, sounds, voices. Some patients say that their 'feelings are on fire,' meaning that which used to be simply pleasant or unpleasant now has assumed gigantic proportions. Now instead of an agreeable sensation, you experience glory itself; instead of the merely unpleasant, you are faced with terrifying, shocking visions or a hopeless sense of impending doom. You go to heaven regularly, or it's the end of the world. You have sensed God or the Devil's presence in your life as never before. Perhaps you feel you have grasped the true meaning of the cosmos, the ever elusive meaning of life. Or you've seen the end of the world, heard angels or devils speaking to you. It's all quite common for people with your condition."

Then he tapped my notebook, which was open on my tray table, with only two blank pages left in the spiral binder.

"Hypergraphia," he said. "A common symptom of the temporal lobe personality. Lots of writing because, of course, God or the Devil is talking and you've got to get it all down. What's a visionary to do with glimpses into the infinite but make a careful record, setting down all of your special insights in excruciating detail for those who do not have such gifts?"

He reached for the notebook. "Do you mind?"

I grabbed the notebook and clasped it to my bosom, then put my channeling crystal on top of it.

"Doesn't matter," he said. "I can assure you we've all had our fill of prolix narratives about divine raptures and heavenly ecstasy before. Haven't we?"

The other doctors didn't nod, because they didn't approve of Stegman's bedside manner, but it was clear that they concurred with his general theories. I was shaking under what amounted to a diagnostic assault.

"I'm a surgeon, madam, not a psychiatrist or a neurologist. I will be the Dutch uncle who gives you the hard facts. Tough love. If you allow these electrical storms to continue raging through your temporal lobe, you will irreparably damage your brain.

"Surgery is a last resort. Our first line of defense is drug therapy, because if we can control the seizure activity with medication, then I won't have to open your nut and go prospecting in there for whatever is causing you to have seizures."

The other doctors solemnly nodded and apparently agreed with everything the medical gorilla had to say. So like it or not, and whether Stegman was an arrogant brute or a genius or both, I had to face the fact that at least five doctors at one of the finest medical establishments in the country felt I had a seizure disorder that needed to be treated. It was as if I had suddenly been told that I had a multiple personality disorder and would be meeting the other people inside me this afternoon.

No matter what was wrong with me, I could no longer bear the arrogant brute who seemed to know everything about my pathology and still managed not to know my first or last name, calling me *madam* instead with maddening regularity.

"Did I mention to you that the Dalai Lama is keenly interested in brain imaging?" I asked.

Dr. Stegman's mouth opened, but nothing came out. At least he stopped writing in his notes. He looked at me even harder and raised an eyebrow.

"Very interesting," he said. "Madam, we are medical scientists. We conduct our medical practice according to reliable data from carefully designed studies."

"Well," I explained, "there are scientific studies showing that people have religious experiences when their temporal lobes are stimulated by magnetic fields. There was a *Newsweek* special issue on it last year called 'Religion and the Brain.' Would you like me to find you a copy?"

"People may or may not have religious experiences," he said. "I don't really care if they do. I am aware of studies showing that some twenty million Americans curtail travel and other major undertakings on Friday the thirteenth.

Does that mean that Friday the thirteenth must therefore ipso facto be unlucky?"

"I believe that your scanning machine captured a powerful religious experience, Dr. Stegman. My faith is very strong."

"You *believe*," he chuckled. "Your faith is very strong. Remind me to give you a tour of our psychiatric ward, madam. I can introduce you to a host of Mad Hatters and March Hares with a wide variety of passionate faiths and beliefs, all of which proves absolutely nothing."

Dr. Nasty didn't wait for a reply. Instead he got up out of his chair, pulled out a digital microrecorder, and began walking away with Metzger.

Stegman dictated as he walked. "Head trauma. Room 959, bed 2."

I saw Dr. Metzger scramble to hold up my chart and point at my name, and Stegman read it. "Mrs. Eleanor Druse. Patient is referred to Dr. Metzger for antiseizure drug therapy and geriatric psychiatric evaluation to rule out senile dementia, with an eye toward perhaps trying her on a course of antipsychotic medications. Patient has had nonclinical epileptic temporal lobe seizures documented by EEG. Her symptoms include depersonalization, flight of ideas, poor reality testing, visual and auditory hallucinations, agitation, hypergraphia, poor hygiene, and religious delusions consistent with temporal lobe personality. Thank you for referring this very interesting patient to our service."

THE FIRE

Bobby went back to Lewiston for three days to work at the Kingdom. Then he surprised me by taking a vacation day and driving back down to see me. Such a sweet boy to look after his mum. He brought me a jar of my favorite Hawaiian white honey from the organic food store down the street. Such a thoughtful gift. I really did try to focus on the white honey, instead of dwelling on how I'd asked him to find out as much as he could about the fire that burned the old Kingdom Hospital to the ground when I was still a little girl. I'd told him that I needed to know about the fire so I could decipher Madeline Kruger's cryptic note to me the night she'd died. *The little girl who saved us is still lost. The fire did not kill her.*

Not only had I asked Bobby for information, I had followed up with explicit suggestions about how and where he might find out about the fire and any little girls that almost died in it. I had reminded him that I was still an emeritus professor at Faust College, and that the librarian, Judy Harris, would be happy to dig up the history of the old hospital and the fire. Or what about the Lewiston *Sun Journal?* How far back do their archives go? Somebody's got to have access to back issues of the old Lewiston *Daily Sun.*

Did Bobby do any of those things? Did he bring me a shred of paper representing even a token attempt at research? No. He devoted all of five minutes to investigating the fire. On his coffee break, he wandered down to the medical library and asked Mr. Benjamin Bates, the librarian, if he knew anything about the fire that burned the old hospital to the ground some time in the 1930s. The frustrations of being a parent never end! I charged the boy with finding out *everything he could* about the fire. Instead, he returned to Boston and made the following report:

"Mum, the old Kingdom Hospital burned down on November second, 1939. No little girls died in the fire. Only two people died. Some old doctor and a boy."

"That's the date on Madeline's note, Bobby! The same one she wrote in the hospital the night she died. All Souls' Day. My birthday! How did the fire start, Bobby? How about names? Did you get their names?"

A blank look on his face.

"How would I know how the fire started? Whose names, Mum?"

"The doctor's name or the little boy's name? The people who died in the fire."

"Uh, no, Mum. What do you want with their names? That was sixty some years ago. Mr. Bates said the old doctor was famous for doing some kind of psychological surgery. That, and pain research."

"The Pain Room," I said without knowing why I said it or where I'd heard of it. It just popped out of my mouth. "The Pain Room," like the familiar name of a person whose face I had long ago forgotten, along with the circumstances of how and why I knew the name. It happens a lot in old age. Somebody asks you if you know Bob Miller. You know the name, but that's all. Maybe fifty or sixty years ago, you knew Bob Miller's face, the names of his children, his favorite authors and movies. Now nothing's left but Bob Miller, a familiar-sounding name.

"The Pain Room. Have you heard of it before?"

"No, Mum."

"The Pain Room."

I had the familiar sensation of feeling my way along a black wall in a dark corridor, searching for a fingerhold, a peephole, a passageway, an opening, a way in.

"Train Sourball Laboratory," I said.

Bobby opened his mouth and looked at me as if I had just spoken Mandarin Chinese.

"Mum, what are you doing? What are you saying?"

"I don't know," I confessed. "It was just like Pain Room. It just popped out. They're just words, Bobby, and they made a little salad of themselves. I don't know why they came out just then."

"I think you're on the train to the oddball laboratory, Mum. Are you sure you don't want to try some of those pills they want you to take?"

NANCY CONLAN'S SECRET

Stegman's visit introduced me to a new sensation: chest pains. The megalomaniacal prana radiating from a single ambient brain surgeon managed to disrupt seventy-five years of coronary calm. I leave it to the cardiologists of tomorrow to design prospective, randomized, placebo-controlled, double-blind trials that will establish that malignant force fields given off by the likes of Stegman can indeed scramble the electrical conductivity of a healthy heart and induce deadly arrhythmias. I drew my own privacy curtain — not something anybody would ever expect of me — and hid in my bed to ponder my treatment alternatives. I tried to ignore the grotesque sounds coming from Nancy's side of the room.

Stegman's visit seemed to have unsettled her as well. She had been making strange croodling noises, gasping, lunging, rattling the bedrails with her restraints. A particularly violent banging brought me up out of my bed and prompted me to look through the curtain to see if the poor thing needed my help.

Her restraints had more slack than usual, and Nancy had managed somehow to bring her wrist close enough to her mouth so that her teeth were fastened on the tie-line of the restraint. Her eyes still rolled listlessly to one side and stared at the floor, but she growled and chewed on the restraint like a trapped wolverine gnawing its paw off to escape a snare.

"Poor, poor child," I said.

I stroked her hair and brow and soothed her by humming to her. She slumped back lifelessly onto her pillow, but her jaw remained locked and her teeth embedded in the cords of the restraint.

"Dear child," I said. "Poor Nancy."

I turned on her call light, and of course no one came for at least twenty minutes. Understaffed, as usual. Finally Tiffany showed and tried a number of feckless maneuvers to unfasten Nancy's teeth from the restraint. She wrapped a damp washcloth around Nancy's nose and mouth, hoping the poor woman would unclench her teeth long enough to gasp for a breath, but Nancy simply seethed and sucked air right through and around the barrier, her eyes wild and her chest heaving with effort, but her teeth firmly embedded in the mesh of the cord. Jennifer came in to help and untied the restraint, replacing it with a new one, and leaving the old one in Nancy's mouth like a chew toy.

It was two hours before Nancy fell asleep and her jaw unhinged and sagged ajar to its resting state. Tiffany was able to remove the cord, now soaked in saliva, scarred and punctured by teeth marks.

After Tiffany left, I stood at the foot of Nancy's bed, unable to look away from her. I prayed for her and her family. I felt like the faithful who cut a hole in the roof and lowered the paralytic down to where the Human-born one was preaching. *Lord, here's our sister, poor Nancy. She's afflicted and suffering. Please help me find a way to help her.*

"She's almost exactly my age."

The voice made me jump and clutch my chest. I turned and saw nurse Claudia standing just behind me. She dabbed at a stray tear with a Kleenex, her eyes reddening again with that same changeable sadness.

"Claudia. You threw a fright into me!"

"There's the fright," she said, nodding toward Nancy Conlan, or what was once a person so named. "She has three children, almost the same ages as mine. Her husband, almost the same age. Same, same, same." Claudia wept quietly, then finally broke down entirely and buried her face in her hands.

I prayed I had the power to allay whatever sorrow was afflicting Claudia. She had a good heart and a gentle disposition.

I reached out and touched her. "There, there, dear. We can't bear such tragedy alone, we have to turn it over to the Divinity who absorbs all. Trust God. You believe, don't you?"

She nodded and went on. "All I had to do was warn her. The same as I tried to warn you. But I didn't. I was afraid that she and her family — She was a checkout clerk at a grocery store in South Boston. Her husband is a laborer for a drywall contractor. Simple, good people. I was afraid they were so *simple* that they might let slip that a nurse had warned them away from —"

"From what, dear?"

"What I wanted to tell you the day before yesterday, before Dr. Metzger interrupted us, Sally, was that if you end up needing surgery, you must not let Dr. Stegman perform the operation."

I looked again at the mute, flesh-fallen frame and the hollow face of a mother whose children were growing up without her.

"Stegman did this?" I gasped, clutching at my crystal necklace. The grave would be a better place for her. Better death than to live on as a bedridden zombie, a constant reminder of what once was.

"Is he incompetent?" I asked. "Is he a butcher?"

She shook her head. "On the contrary, he's brilliant. Probably the most skilled neurosurgeon on staff, and that's his problem. He never says no. His patient load grows every year — always has. He runs clinic and surgery on the same day. Sometimes both at once. Scrubbing in and out as needed. He leaves his fellows at work on one case while he runs out and starts another or zips over to the clinic for a quick consult. Then half an hour later, he scrubs back into the same procedure."

"That can't be."

"It's illegal, Mrs. Druse. Against hospital rules. He's infected with the MORE virus: more patients, more procedures, more research, more prestige, more money. More. More. More. And patients like poor Nancy are the casualties of his runaway ambition. They suffer because there's no more time in his day to do a careful job of anything anymore. He just does the best he can under the circumstances, which are always frantic, chaotic, overwhelming."

"What did he do to her?"

"He operated on the wrong side of her brain, and then tried to claim it was because he'd seen a second lesion on the scans before beginning surgery. The film's conveniently missing, but he swears on it. Now she's in what's called a persistent vegetative state — eyes open, permanent unconsciousness. According to the EEGs, she sleeps and wakes up, but she's totally unaware of herself and her environment. Her brain stem functions, but the PET scans show almost no cortical activity. She can't chew or swallow, because you need intact cerebral hemispheres for that. She's been like this for months."

"And he's still doing surgery?" I had trouble fathoming how this could be so.

"I told you: He is a brilliant surgeon. Still is, but he's unraveling now under the pressure of the self-inflicted overload. He generates millions in revenue doing arguably unnecessary procedures, which he defends by saying that he aggressively protects the health of his patients. Yes, it's true that for the last few months, maybe even for the last year, he's been the star of the mortality and morbidity conferences. Meaning the lawsuits will soon follow. But until he costs them more than he generates in revenue, tragedies like this will continue happening."

"It can't continue. He must be stopped."

"That won't happen anytime soon. It'll continue until the lawsuits mount or the medical licensing board investigates."

"Who else knows what this man has been doing?"

"I know a lot because he likes using our unit for his patients. We've seen several like this, and several complaints followed."

Silence. She looked at the floor and sniffled.

"The complaints did nothing?" I asked. "He's still practicing?"

"Yes, and the nurses who complained were fired. That's why I can't — So now, instead of complaining afterwards, I warn people I trust *before*."

"Does her family know?"

Claudia shook her head. "They know and they don't know. They know something went wrong, but they are too trusting. They don't know enough medicine, let alone neurology, to ask the right questions. They are barely able to grasp what's happened."

"Monstrous!" I cried, looking at the poor woman who was now a prisoner in her own slowly deteriorating body.

"Not only is he responsible for her condition,

the bastard is keeping her alive on top of it. He's against withdrawing the tube feedings."

"What does the family say?"

"Depends which family you talk to and whether they've just spoken to Stegman. Nancy's husband, Dave, and his mother, Virginia, want the tube out. They want to let Nancy go. They know she'll never recover."

"What do her parents say?"

"Whatever Stegman tells them to say. He's got the hospital's neurologists in his pocket, and gets at least two of them to say that Nancy's CAT scans and MRI scans are ambiguous and that the metabolic rate of glucose uptake in the cerebral hemispheres, although diminished, does not conclusively indicate a total loss of cerebral cortical function. Blah, blah, blah."

"Who cares about tests?" I argued. "Just look. She's no longer alive in any meaningful sense of the word. She's not there. Her body is, but her soul is gone."

"He's got a video clip somebody took with a digital camera that shows Nancy lifting her head, supposedly in response to the presence of others in the room."

"It's not right to put her family through this," I said.

"Sally," Claudia said, and her eyes reddened again with guilty tears, "please. You mustn't let on that I told you anything. Or —"

"I know, I know," I said. "Don't worry."

DRUG THERAPY

The next day Dr. Metzger arranged to meet with me in the early morning on the neurology ward. Tiffany showed me into a conference room, where I was surprised to find that the butcher psychiatrist had enlisted the services of a secret ally.

"Hello, Sally," said Claudia. She looked a little sheepish, as if she'd wanted to warn me ahead of time about this meeting but had been instructed otherwise.

Metzger had changed back into his clinical white lab coat, complete with pocket protectors and badges. He looked pleased with himself and quickly apologized for his superior's abysmal behavior of the day previous.

"Dr. Stegman means well," he said, "but like many surgeons, he's not a people person." Big smile.

If he's a person at all, I thought. So far I thought of Stegman as exhibit A in the case against materialism: No mere collection of cells, molecules, and atoms could be so hateful. The man's physical body was but a conveyance for his infinitely malevolent spirit.

"Dr. Stegman is often overly direct," Metzger continued. "He is concerned about you, as am I. And I enlisted Claudia's help, because I know she's worried about you, too."

Claudia nodded. "Sally, Dr. Metzger asked me to help him convince you that it is in your best interest to do something about the seizure activity that you may be having according to your EEGs."

"I don't like medications," I said. "If there's something wrong with my brain, I'd rather do some of my own woo-woo on it and make it go away. If there's healing to be done, I'll do it myself."

"Drug therapy completely eliminates seizures in a third of patients," said Metzger, "and greatly reduces the frequency of seizures in another third. As for woo-woo, I'm not aware of any studies —"

"If your seizures go untreated," said Claudia, "you could have another bad fall, or the seizures could get progressively worse until they start causing mental deterioration. And with a wonderful mind like yours, Sally, we don't want that."

"Sometimes patients like their seizures," said Metzger. "Conversely they don't like the drugs, because the drugs make them overly sedated, spacey, or dizzy. For instance, some say that certain seizure medications make them feel slightly drunk. We have a new drug protocol I'd like you to enroll in. The exciting thing is that it may not just suppress any seizure activity, but may also enhance your mystical experiences."

"Enhanced mystical experiences?" I asked. "Is it cut with psilocybin, ayahuasca, LSD?"

"Bad girl," he said. "I've found literature that suggests patients have an enhanced state of well-being, and" — he smiled at me — "how did you put it? A sensitivity to wonder and to the unity of all beings and things?"

"Patients are allowed to make bad decisions," said Claudia. "We can't force you to take any medicine. We can only give you the facts."

Claudia was melting me with daughterly concern, and I was wondering if perhaps I shouldn't give their medicines a try and see what might come of it.

"We want to try you on Scyllazine," said Metzger. "It's an antiepileptic. Sometimes there are side effects, in which case we administer Charybdisol to counteract those. But the good thing about Scyllazine is that there are far fewer side effects of the sort that usually trouble an active and spirited person like yourself, Mrs. Druse."

"Well . . ." I said. "If I start taking the stuff, will you let me go home to Lewiston?"

Claudia smiled.

Metzger said, "We'll just keep you here until we establish proper serum levels of the drug and get your dosages all straightened out. I bet we can send you home to Maine within a week."

Claudia saw the look on my face and gave me a big kiss.

Bring on the drugs.

The trick to handling doctors is to steer them into ordering tests that will provide useful information, then keep yourself in charge of your own care. Otherwise they have a way of imposing their own push-pull, cause-effect view of the universe on your own precious etheric body. In this case, I was willing to give them the benefit of the doubt.

I haven't always been so medically manageable. In 1972, at the age of forty-four, I sat across the table from Dr. Cherilyn Crabb, a Kingdom Hospital oncologist, in an examination room at the Kingdom clinics and received a death sentence. They had found blood in my urine, and then Dr. Crabb had found renal cell cancer — a three-centimeter mass in my right kidney and quarter-sized metastases to my lungs. Dr. Crabb said that they would go in and take out the kidney, as a strictly palliative measure, but that the metastases in my lungs were untreatable. Her advice was that I should go home after surgery and put my affairs in order, because the median survival rate for patients with Stage IV renal cell cancer was less than one year, and I had an 8 percent chance of living two years.

Dr. Crabb even showed me a chart of two-year survival rates for the various stages and types of renal cell cancer, with a little X penciled in the Stage IV column where the bar graph fell somewhat short of 8 and was actually closer to 7.

I let them take the kidney, but then I went right to work on treating myself. I switched to an entirely macrobiotic diet, meditated daily, and used guided imagery meditation to visualize the cancer in my lungs. I summoned my immune system to destroy it.

One night I was deep in prayer, and yes, very afraid that God would touch me with his finger and take me from this world — a single mother with seven-year-old Bobby to look after. I was deep in prayer asking for nothing less than the usual: "Dear Lord, please annul the laws of medical science on my behalf and allow me to live."

It was the one and only time (until recently) that I sensed a true presence. If it was God, He appeared to me not as a father or an angel, but as a huge formless presence towering and looming over me, beyond my ken or the powers of my mortal sense to conform Him to a recognizable shape. Instead, some part of Him reached out and touched my chest.

I guess the end of that story is pretty obvious. I've gotten along fine with one kidney, and the lung metastases went away like a bad cold.

Six months later, the ghostly white quarters were all gone from my X-ray. God had touched me, and I lived.

SOMA

Madeline Kruger's note had me stumped, as did all the talk of the little girl. Still lost? Back in the lair of the living? One reason I decided to let them give me pills was fear. I was afraid that I was missing a chunk of memory. A block of brain cells that had recorded whatever I had shared so long ago with Madeline was gone. Senile dementia? Or was it the progressive effects of the seizures they'd been warning me about? According to the doctors, I could have been having them for years. Each one draining the batteries of my brain cells and depleting stores of memories. Including, maybe, whatever Evil had touched Madeline and me, and all about the lost little girl.

Bobby had been bringing me Lewiston *Sun Journals* from home, which were scattered around on my bed and nightstand. A few headlines caught my eye.

"Licensing Board Investigates Medical Fatality."

It wasn't on the front page, but it was prominently placed at the top of the local news section, and it described the death of little Theresa Bradley, eight years old, following a routine procedure to repair her pulmonary valve. This was the little girl Bobby had told me about who died the same night Madeline did at the Kingdom. Full moon, Friday the thirteenth. A separate story described how the girl's mother, Sarah Bradley, was being charged with assault for attacking the pediatric cardiologist with a surgical scalpel.

Alongside were photos of little Theresa and the physician, Dr. Edward Egas, who not only got forty stitches out of the deal but was also under investigation after the procedure had ended in the fatal injury to the child's heart.

I tore out those stories and tucked them into my notebooks. Then I saw one more. A story that was obviously buried as far back as possible. Not the back page — worse, inside the back page, at the bottom:

"Ringing Hospital Bell Blamed On Malfunctioning Elevator Chimes."

The story described how in the wee hours of Friday, December 13 (the night of Madeline's death and of my episode), during and after a number of disturbances, which included a minor earthquake and several medical emergencies, witnesses at Kingdom Hospital reported hearing the sound of a bell ringing throughout the hospital. A nurse found the ringing bell so peculiar and ubiquitous that she summoned two *Sun Journal* reporters and a Lewiston police officer, who were met by several other baffled hospital employees and led to the hospital elevators, where the sounds of the ringing bell were especially loud and pronounced. "Insistent," in the words of one witness.

Investigators blamed the disturbances on malfunctioning elevator chimes, even though, when interviewed separately, elevator repairmen on the scene said that all power was cut to the elevators during and after the earthquake, and that the chimes do not function without electricity.

Kingdom Hospital administrator Jesse James, architect of the medical center's progressive new Operation Morning Air corporate wellness program, attributed the reports of bells ringing to malfunctioning elevator chimes and to stress in the workplace. "The employees of Kingdom Hospital work very hard 24-7 to deliver quality medical care to Lewiston and surrounding communities."

End of story. I knew the ringing bell meant something. I knew it was connected with everything that had happened that night. Knew it as surely as I knew that I had traveled between life and death the night of Madeline Kruger's death. I'm ashamed to admit it, but what I did was . . . nothing.

I settled back against my pillow and drifted off into the hospitable glow of Scyllazine, 100 milligrams, twice daily.

I didn't have the heart to tell Claudia, but the medications promptly deprived me of my ability to give myself over to the flow of my daily meditations. When I closed my eyes and waited for the familiar tug of the current that runs through the entire universe, nothing happened. But there was a consolation prize: I didn't really care. Just like I didn't care that the ringing bell meant something and nobody was going to investigate it, because it was easier to blame it on unplugged elevator chimes and workplace stress.

The pills had other effects. When Tiffany or

Jennifer or Nancy's family came to visit, I felt strangely tentative and uncertain, but without the mild anxiety that I expected would attend such a state — like being shy without feeling self-conscious, if such a thing is possible. This was only one paradox in a mental state that seemed constructed of such paradoxes. When the medication reached peak concentration, I felt unwilling or unable to act or speak but also satisfied with my condition — not happy or joyful, by any means, but also not concerned, as if thinking or taking action were not quite worth the trouble, because actions might lead to worry or regret.

My inner mental state seemed to be packaged in Styrofoam peanuts, protected from the buffets and accidents of the outside world. It was quite the opposite of the unitary state of enlightenment that I'd aspired to my whole life, a oneness with nature and the entire universe. Instead, the meds induced a kind of accentuated duality, one in which my insular inner self was protected from the slings and arrows of outraged fortune by neurochemical bubble wrap. The predominant sensation was that I was calm, if not at peace, and that the safest thing to do was always nothing, or at least as little as possible. Less risk, and an increased chance of maintaining the satisfactory status quo.

As an academic, I felt the pills would be ideal for C students. They would remove the vanity, discontent, and restlessness that motivates a C student to try for a B or an A. They would also remove the anxiety of not trying hard enough and incurring a D or F. Thus a C was satisfactory, the aim and end-state of the perfect medication.

For several days, I sat in my own drug-induced private Idaho and realized that I had only to take a pill each day and I could remain forever in this limbo state of not exactly happy and not exactly sad. Another troublesome, loopy, time-consuming old biddy of a patient neutralized and rendered as contented as an oyster in her shell, while my insurance company went on making regular payments.

INSTANT KARMA

Soon my days were all the same, muddy and indistinct, each one flowing into the next. I was repeatedly warned to stay on my medication and to cooperate with the physicians or my insurance might not cover the entire cost of my care. I decided to take the pills long enough to obtain an honorable discharge from Boston General.

Very early one morning, I heard Tiffany and Jennifer giggling behind the curtain about Dr. Stegman. For just a second (probably a side effect of the accursed medication), I was stumped. I knew that name, Stegman, but I couldn't remember how or why. Then a visceral

111

nausea erupted in the vicinity of my second chakra (abdomen and lower back), as if the flow there had been suddenly blocked. His name alone was a positive energy sink, a drain on my élan vital, before the rest of me could even remember who he was.

As I pieced together snatches of the nurses' chatter, I learned that they had arrived earlier than usual with extra toiletries to give Nancy a special bath and to wash and fix her hair, with a nice blue ribbon. I heard them whispering about a yeast infection in the poor woman's mouth. "Oral thrush," Jennifer called it. And they made each other take turns swabbing the infection with something called methylene blue. They must have assumed I was senile or deaf or well medicated and couldn't hear them whispering, "Ew, gross," or "Yuck," or "I can't look at it anymore, you do it." The chorus continued through the debriding of the woman's pressure sores and the insertion of a brand new catheter tube and feeding tube and fresh clean cotton wrist restraints.

Toward the end of it all, I heard Stegman's name again and learned the reason for this early morning overhaul of Nancy Conlan and her appurtenances. Stegman was presenting Nancy to an army of physicians in something called Grand Rounds. She was to be poked and prodded, tested and examined in an effort to determine if she had indeed progressed to a permanent condition the medical experts referred to as a persistent vegetative state, a diagnosis that would allow the family, in consultation with the hospital and its physicians, to discontinue tube feedings and withdraw nutrition.

Mornings were Nancy's worst time anyway, and this morning she seemed especially restless, banging her bound hands against the bedrails, pitching forward on occasion and making a gagging sound, then throwing her head back and searching the walls behind her head with the whites of her eyes. To me it seemed that as her brain damage progressed, her body operated almost of its own accord, like a headless chicken or a pithed frog.

The nurses said that Stegman had specifically ordered that Nancy be given no medications or sedatives because he wanted her as "alert" as possible for the conference — a notion that made the nurses titter derisively. So Nancy's random flailing and spastic gasping had gotten steadily worse since last night. No doubt Stegman was planning on bringing in his minions, clapping his hands, and seeing if the poor girl would sit up and bark like a seal. "There, you see?" he would say. "She's responsive. How can we withdraw nutrition from a responsive patient with her whole life ahead of her?"

I only hoped that the man whose personal demons had run amok and brought misery and ruin to Nancy and her entire family would have this pathetic creature's image burned into his memory and then carry it foremost in his mind all the way to the grave.

At eight sharp, Dr. Stegman marched in with twenty or so physicians, medical residents, and interns in tow. First they surrounded my bed. I had a terrible headache and my brain floated in the usual suspended animation.

Dr. Stegman asked how I was tolerating the medications.

I felt as if someone else was doing the talking, but a part of my brain had miraculously retained the ability to speak the truth according to the Gospel of St. Matthew.

"The eye is the body's lamp," I said. "If your eyes are good, your body will be filled with light; if your eyes are bad, your body will be in darkness. And if your light is darkness, how deep will the darkness be!"

Stegman turned to a pretty medical resident and said, "Religious ideations still prominent. Make a note of it."

Then he turned back to me and said, "Go on. Please continue. Don't mind us."

"The pills cloud my eyes. They dim the light. When my eyes are bad, my body is in darkness."

Stegman fetched out his digital recorder and paced as he spoke into it. "Room 959, bed two, a Mrs. —"

The pretty med student held up the chart, a candy-red fingernail on the name tag.

"— Drusey. Complains that the Scyllazine 100 milligrams B.I.D. induces a state of semi-

114

voluntary apraxia. Also complaining of vision problems. Refer to Dr. Burt in ophthalmology to rule out macular degeneration and cataracts."

Stegman smiled a tight one my way, then waved his troops over to the next bed for the main event.

Tiffany tried to pull the privacy curtain shut, but she inadvertently left an opening between the curtain's border and the wall, which meant I could still see Nancy's head thrown back on the pillow, grimacing, making those terrible gagging and laughing sounds. She lurched spastically and her head lunged forward at nothing.

Stegman presided over the ceremonies like a showman displaying a circus freak. He rattled off diseases, syndromes, and sequelae; lab values, diagnostic scan findings, and test results. He moved to the head of the bed, where he shined a penlight in each of Nancy's eyes and said, "Oculogyric crisis." He indicated her dead-bird claw hands and said, "Contractures."

The other doctors took careful notes and murmured "Interesting" or "Very interesting" upon hearing about her uremia or her white cell count or her elevated pH.

At this point, Stegman motioned for Tiffany to unfasten Nancy's restraints so that he could move her arms. He demonstrated the range of motion of her shriveled limbs, tugging her this way and that while describing her interesting defects in Latin, using words like *dyskinesia* or

115

torticollis, posing now and again to receive the admiration of the female residents.

Then Stegman put a latex glove on his right hand, and Tiffany gave him a tongue depressor, which he used to probe Nancy's mouth.

One by one the eager young medical scientists were treated to a view of Nancy's very interesting clinical example of oral thrush, a kind of white fur growing inside her mouth which, from the looks on their faces, must have been enough to make Job question his faith.

I believe God or Satan provided me with a sudden premonition of what was about to happen. I suppose the other possibility is that I actually caused it to happen, by some as yet unexplained psychokinetic stimulation of the motor areas of what was left of Nancy Conlan's brain. Precognition, or just good old-fashioned instinct shining through the medicinal fog, I don't know which, but I knew it was coming and I can't say I didn't relish the prospect.

Stegman used the tongue depressor to move aside the flap of Nancy's cheek, so that yet another shameless professional voyeur of her pathology could feast his or her eyes on the manifold pleasures of the grotesque. Nancy suddenly lurched forward, opened her mouth in a hideous grimace, then clamped her teeth onto the gloved hand of Dr. Stegman. As I watched in horrified delight, I could see that the purchase her teeth had obtained on the meat of his right palm was at least as tenacious and forceful as the one she'd had on the cotton wrist restraint some days previous.

Stegman howled in agony and gingerly attempted to withdraw his hand — "Ow, OW, OW, OWWWW!" — without leaving a piece of it behind in Nancy's incisors, but he succeeded only in tugging her head up off the pillow. Her wide-open eyes swelled and flushed red in their sockets and her facial muscles bulged and flexed as her jaws locked and exerted increasing force on her teeth, which sank deeper, through the membrane of the glove, through the skin, and into the flesh of Stegman's hand.

Dark blood filled the semitransparent latex glove and then streamed in rivulets from the holes made by her teeth and dribbled around her lips and chin.

Stegman howled louder and pulled again at his trapped hand, but it only brought Nancy up off the pillow and closer to his screaming face. She lurched again and her claw hands fastened onto his lab coat, those bony talons grasping the lapels with the blind fury of raw motor automatism. Now she had ahold of him, tooth and claw, and his panic was pure. He tried to step back, which had the effect of dragging her into a half-sitting position on the frame of the bedrails, from which she tipped forward and clung to him.

Stegman tripped on his heels and fell back, dragging Nancy down on top of him, her teeth still firmly embedded in the flesh of his hand.

She was growling and gnawing and clinging to him with the relentless vigor of unguided reflex-driven musculature. She was like a human drone missile who had found its target.

The other physicians tried to help, but what could they do? Any attempt to pull Nancy off their leader caused him to shriek, "Don't pull on her, damn it! She'll take half my hand with her!"

Jennifer and Tiffany hurried over and helped me out of bed.

"Mrs. Druse," said Tiffany, "this is an emergency situation. We are going to move you out into the hall so that the emergency team can bring in the crash cart and give Nancy some special medicine so she'll let go of Dr. Stegman's hand."

I can't say for sure, but I may have seen laughter in their eyes.

NOBLE SAVAGERY

By late afternoon, things had calmed down, and I was able to return to my bed. I'd missed my morning medication and felt my head clearing, so I took the occasion to review my recent notes, most of which I couldn't remember from day to day.

I found one dated two days back that read: "Dr. Stegman visited this morning and seemed pleasant and agreeable. He still doesn't remember my name, but it's probably because he's so busy trying to help all of his patients. He works too hard, but I believe he is well-intentioned. Remember to ask Claudia if he is really a bad man or just a victim of circumstances."

My last dose had been yesterday afternoon, so the soma fog (as I had come to call the effects of the Scyllazine) had lifted, and I read with horror those words I couldn't remember writing. I heard Nancy gag in the next bed.

If Metzger kept his promise, I had only three days left before Bobby would drive me back to Lewiston. I had things to do first, and they weren't going to get done if I was sitting around barmy on pharmaceuticals and writing love notes to the likes of Stegman.

I cheeked my next two doses and flushed them down the toilet after lights out. Next day I did the same.

It was easy to pretend that I was still medicated. All I had to do was nothing, and no matter what happened or what anyone said to me, all I had to say was "That's fine" or "I don't care."

Claudia came in to advise that Stegman's hand had been mutilated and infected with a deadly bacteria called clostridium, famous for causing gas gangrene. Human bites are apparently far worse than the bite of any other animal except poisonous snakes and rabid dogs. Claudia said that cultures taken of wounds caused by human bites are polymicrobial, yielding an average of five microorganisms cultured per wound. She said that streaks of red had appeared on Stegman's arm within hours of the bite and had traveled rapidly up above his elbow. He'd spiked a temperature and shown the classical symptoms of cellulitis.

"How awful," I said.

"Then came the smell," said Claudia.

"The smell?" I asked.

"Progressive myonecrosis," she said. "The bacteria produces a gas that gets trapped inside the skin. Hence the name: gas gangrene. But its most distinguishing feature is its odor. It smells like a dead guy eating a mustard gas sandwich in a World War I trench."

"Is there a cure?" I asked. Claudia was already gloating and didn't need any help from me. If Stegman was about to lose an arm to gas gangrene, I was almost ready to feel sorry for him.

"They had to open the flesh of his arm along the fascial planes of the muscles and clean out the bacterial infection. Then they put him on IV antibiotics. It doesn't look like he'll lose an arm. Unfortunately. He may even live to operate on someone else."

"The poor man," I said. And blessed myself, mainly because I didn't know what else to do.

"Yes," said Claudia. "Poor man. Actually I was hoping for a diagnosis of necrotizing fasciitis. The one the tabloids call the flesh-eating bacterium. Could have killed him by now, and Boston General would be a safe hospital again."

I patted her hand.

"There now, Claudia," I said. "Forgiveness is the best revenge."

THE CRYSTAL SPEAKS

Nancy's parents, Renn and Margie, came in that weekend to see what had happened to their little girl. The doctors had given Nancy IV muscle relaxants and sedatives, because it had been the only way to free Stegman's hand from her snapping-turtle jaws.

She was asleep on the pillow, eyes closed, more peaceful than I had ever seen her.

I held a Selene crystal in front of me on a silk string, and used it as a pendulum to determine how I might help Claudia and Nancy and her family out of the disaster that their lives had become. At Renn's request, I took out the channeling crystal and agreed to ask it for guidance on his behalf.

"Can you ask it if my little girl will ever wake up again? Be her old self?"

"I don't know," I said. "I'll try to ask it."

"Wait," he said, and touched my hand to stop me. He swallowed hard and got red around the eyes. "Wait a sec. Maybe I don't want to know."

"Go ahead on and ask it," said Margie. Her

jaw was set, ready for whatever the crystal might say.

I looked at Renn again and he nodded.

The pendulum slowed very gradually and began oscillating slightly sideways. I saw it blur through my own tears and my hand shook.

"She will not," I said. "She will never walk or talk again. She will never be the same old Nancy. She's gone."

I wept freely. Renn and Margie joined me. I was afraid he would be angry with me, but instead he seemed relieved.

He touched my free hand. "Thank you."

"Wait," I said, studying the quartz moving at the end of my string. "That's not all."

"What?" he asked, trembling, leaning closer. "What is it?"

"This terrible thing that happened to your daughter," I said, studying the crystal's movement. "It was not meant to be."

Renn frowned and wiped his eyes. He balled up his red fists. "What does that mean? Not meant to be? I wasn't meant to be washing pots and pans at Rudy's Fish House, but I am. What do I do with 'not meant to be'?"

"I mean to say that according to the crystal pendulum, there was a serious medical error made during your daughter's surgery. That's why she is the way she is. Someone made a terrible mistake."

"Well, what am I supposed to do about that?" asked Renn, gripping my bedrails, trying to fathom this new view of the medical solar system he'd just glimpsed by way of the crystal. "What do I do about the mistake now? It's done."

"You need to — Wait, let me concentrate."

I watched the pendulum change directions. Now it was swinging vigorously in an arc that drew Renn and me together in a kind of temporary dyad.

"Yes, it's just as I thought," I said. "It's really very simple."

"What?" he asked. "Tell me, Mrs. Druse, what?"

"You need to go see a very good medical malpractice lawyer."

"I do?" asked Renn.

"Yes," I said. "According to the crystal, a good plaintiffs' lawyer will tell you exactly what to do."

RETURN TO THE KINGDOM

THE CONDITION OF THE BODY

It was undiluted pleasure to go back home to Maine. Seizure or no seizures, near death or far from it, out of body or marooned inside this old bag of bones — be it ever so humble, there's no place like being back behind the windows of my old house and the eyes of my mended body.

Health is a golden crown we all wear, but we can't see it until we get sick. Getting well again bestows a renewed appreciation for the tiniest delights, the most uncontrived comforts. I went into my own kitchen and made myself a pot of tea. The wooden handle of my favorite cane felt like an old friend's warm handshake. I purged the lingering odors of Bobby's pipe smoke, beer, and pizza using bindles of sage and a potpourri. I sat in my favorite chair by the window and let our mixed-breed pound dog, Skipper, mostly lab with a little spaniel and who knows what all, put his snout in my lap and nuzzle me a warm hello.

"Good boy, Skip."

What is life but a struggle to find a safe warm corner of the world where one can turn around three times, settle down for a moment's rest, and think: *Well, I'm happy and healthy, at least for now.* But in all honesty, my home of thirty-some years no longer felt like the most intimate surroundings on the planet. The last ten days made the most familiar objects of my old life — my books and reading glasses, my ottoman and end table, the antique lamp my mother left me — seem as changeable and insubstantial as spirits. I expected them to melt or grow lips and whisper to me at any moment.

I was seized by a vague fear, as if instead of being back, I was actually far away in a foreign land where I didn't speak the language or know the customs. I felt like an expatriate in Saudi Arabia, who creates an illusory, artificial, little Americanized apartment inside a secure compound, where she can pretend to be safe at home in familiar surroundings, even though she knows that just outside the walls are rag-headed mobs ready to stone her to death for sleeping with the wrong man.

The date of departure from my comfortable past to the uncertain, alien present? December thirteenth, the night Madeline Kruger died.

I grabbed an old Lewiston-Auburn phone book and my reading glasses and looked up Werling. Laurel Werling. The nurse who had led me into Madeline's room that terrible night. I'd written down her name the minute Bobby had reminded me of it in Boston. And the orderly's name was Angelo Charron.

I found Werling, L., out on Lyngby Road. I copied her name, address, and phone onto a yellow sticky. I dialed the number, and my heart jumped in my throat when I recognized Laurel's chipper voice on the recorded greeting: "Hi, it's me, leave a message and I'll call you back."

"Ms. Werling," I said, "this is Eleanor Druse, Sally Druse, we met almost two weeks ago on the Kingdom Hospital psychiatric ward where you . . . were working. I had an episode of some kind that night. I guess you must know that. I'm sure you do. Anyway, I have some questions I'd like to ask you about what happened, if you wouldn't mind calling me back."

I left my phone number for her and went back to the phone book, where I found no listing for Charron or any alternate spelling thereof. Next I found Kruger, M., still at the address where she'd lived for decades: 519 Woodlawn. Walking distance but for the snow outside. I rested my hand on the phone and stared at the number. I'm always at my best in person, so I considered bundling up in my wool sweater and coat and driving over there in my old Volvo. It was a one-and-a-half-story Pennsylvania Dutch bungalow, as I recalled. If Hilda Kruger was still in town handling Madeline Kruger's estate, I could go see her in person. But if I showed up unannounced, it might put her on the defensive, especially if I started asking questions about her mother's death or trying to get my hands on that suicide note.

I mulled over how to proceed. Perhaps I should just phone and express my condolences first? I could get to know Hilda and make her realize that her mom and I were friends a very long time ago, that there was obviously something important she wanted me to know. Had her mother, for instance, ever spoken about being saved by a little girl? Or a lost little girl? Or a fire?

Nobody answered at the Krugers' and there was no answering machine or service either, so I could decide about how to proceed on that front later.

I gathered up the newspapers and took them out to my sitting room, where I could read and look out the window at the winter light sparkling in the icicles and snowdrifts.

Bobby had worked nights as usual, and I heard him coming down the back steps to the kitchen, where he foraged for his midafternoon breakfast. I heard him open the cereal cupboard, then rattle a box.

"Mum, the Kommando Krunch is all gone. Did you eat it all?"

"I didn't touch it, Bobby. I've been in the hospital, remember? I don't eat refined carbohydrates. Bleached flour is the staff of death. If you want type two diabetes, put Kommando whosit on the list. I'm going to the store this afternoon."

I heard him set his favorite bowl on the kitchen table where I'd been working and listened to him rustling the inner wrapper of a box of something else. Probably something with sugar and cocoa as the two leading ingredients, if I knew him.

"Mum, what's Laurel Werling's name and phone number doing here?"

"I tried to call her. I want to ask her about the night Madeline died."

The cereal box stopped rustling, and the silence was so conspicuous I could have hung my shawl on it.

"Bobby?"

I didn't need to see him to know that he was sweating — familial pheromones or just plain mother's intuition.

"What's wrong, Bobby?"

Nothing but a long sigh, and the legs of the chair squeaking when he leaned against the back of it for support.

"Mum, Laurel Werling had some kind of nervous breakdown. She's in the Kingdom psych ward."

"She's in the hospital? And you didn't tell me? Bobby!"

I jumped out of my chair and came into the kitchen.

"One bowl of cereal is all you get! And hurry up about it!"

I ran into my bedroom, dressed in my Kingdom smock with my hospice volunteer ID, and bundled up in a wool skirt, sweater, and coat. Then I marched back into the kitchen, all but took him by the ear, dragged him out to the Volvo, and made him drive me to Kingdom Hospital.

I was a common scold all the way to the hospital. In point of fact Bobby doesn't pay attention to anything but violent computer games called Warcraft or Bloodfest or worse. Once I found him hunched over the screen playing something called MDK. "What does that stand for?" I asked. "Murder, Death, Kill," he said, as blasé as you please. I thought he was joking. A grown man indulging in hour upon hour of violent fantasies. No wonder he's still single; he's married to the vixen in Grand Theft Auto.

When I stopped him from pulling out in front of a school bus, he looked at me like it was all my fault, as if I were the one turning left in front of forty children wearing no seat belts.

"Mum, I told you that Laurel Werling got fired."

"Something about overtime?"

"Yes," he said. "So how was I supposed to know that you also wanted me to give you updates on her mental health and medical history? She came in a mess the other night and got a private room. Something about a break. Not a nervous breakdown, a psychological break?"

"Psychotic break," I said.

"There you go, a psychotic break. A personal matter. Would you want me blabbing to every

Nosy Parker if you had a psychosis break and checked into the booby hatch?" This gave him an even better idea. "That stuff is patient information that is privileged under my job description anyhow."

"Quiet, Bobby. Just drive."

We pulled through the loop drive in front of the emergency room entrance, into the parking garage, and down to the lower level, where there was a traffic arm and a big sign that read: EMPLOYEES ONLY. Bobby opened it with a card and we pulled into an empty space.

While we waited at the garage elevators, I noticed two LuvKraft Pest Control trucks parked discreetly in the shadows next to a Ford pickup with a snow-encrusted plow blade on it.

"Bobby, are the earthquakes still causing rodent problems?"

"Oh, yeah, Mum. You name it. Rats, mice, cockroaches, ants."

I gasped. "Ants! Bobby, what ants? You never said a thing about ants. In the winter? The earthquakes are causing ant problems?"

"Sure, Mum. When I told you, I said vermin, didn't I? The earthquakes make the vermin go mad. Didn't I tell you that back in Boston?"

The elevator arrived, but I was so upset I could barely walk into it. Bobby pushed L for the lobby.

"You never said *ants*, Bobby. You said the *rats* got at the bodies. Who's seen ants? Have you seen them?"

"Oh, sure. Otto and I found a hive of them down in an equipment storage room near the old Kingdom. Blondi runs loose down there. We found him barking at a swarm of them that had set up housekeeping in an old IBM server rack."

"What about Madeline Kruger's body? Was it rats or ants that got at it?"

He kept turning away from me on the elevator, and I had a good idea why: He was hiding a pouch of pipe tobacco and pipe cleaners in his coat pocket. When I saw them, I almost went to find the nearest chair and turn him over my knee.

"How would I know what got at her? I wasn't there. I heard the rats got at her. Nobody said a thing about ants."

"Where's the body? Was she cremated?"

"She might still be down there. I heard the family was fighting about how to dispose of her. I told you, Mum, these are hoodoo Catholics. Some of them want her buried in a coffin in a Catholic cemetery, some want her buried at the crossroads with a stake through her heart, and the New Age heretics in the family want her cremated and her ashes sprinkled under the Tree of Life behind the Temple of the Inner Light out on Dimsdale Avenue. There's a court fight going on about it, so I think what's left of her is still down there in the morgue. I know old Ray wants her incinerated because it's cheaper."

Once we made it into the hospital proper, it took us the better part of half an hour to make it up to the psych ward, what with all the nurses and staff asking after my health, wishing me well, welcoming me back home. I made up my mind to stop by the sunshine ward because nurse Liz Hinton told me that my old sweetheart, Lenny Stillmach, was back in, maybe for the last time. His pancreatic cancer was eating him up from the inside out and his housekeeper wasn't able to care for him anymore. He was asking for me. Dear old Lenny. He did what he said he'd do, as usual: They told him he was supposed to be dead six months ago, and he's still here.

We stopped by Otto's security cubicle, where Bobby took a seat in front of the monitors and got mulish on me.

"Go on up there yourself, Mum. I'm not gonna be party to disturbing the peace of some poor mental patient because you want to ask her questions about a suicide. Did it occur to you that it might be a touchy subject with her? It happened on her watch, you know."

Actually, what Bobby wanted was to smoke his pipe in peace without having to hide it from me. It was too awkward to deal with in public. Instead, I left him to his repulsive habit and went to take the elevator to the ninth-floor psych ward. As God is my witness, I was alert and fully in command of my faculties. No daydreams, no auras, no "feelings on fire" or visions of the sort Dr. Mussolini had warned me about.

An elevator arrived with one pretty young woman in a white lab coat. She was holding a tray of syringes and stoppered blood samples and leaning against the rear wall of the car. Behind her, above faux walnut wainscoting, was a wall-sized mirror — a common design ploy to create the illusion of more space in claustrophobic confines. The other walls were the same, with brushed steel handrails below the mirrors. Otherwise the elevator was empty. The girl smiled vaguely and went back to studying a list of patients she had to see.

Two odd occurrences. First: As the elevator passed the seventh floor, the pediatric ward, I heard a child or children crying. I looked at the young woman, but she didn't seem to notice. And the crying seemed to come from above the car, not from the other side of the doors.

The second event was more troubling. The car stopped on eight — one floor up from pediatrics, and one floor down from the psych unit on nine. The doors opened, the pretty young lab technician got out, and no one else got on, or at least I didn't think so. I pushed my number again, even though it was already lit, the way people do out of habit. The next time I looked up, there was an elderly doctor in a clean and starched but frayed lab coat of an unusual style — quite long, with wide, starchy lapels. He was as skinny as a mummy, and his head was covered with a sterile green surgical cap, thick glasses resting on his bony nose. He had his gnarled, age-spotted hands folded in front of him over a faded old brochure that said: "Managing Warfarin (Coumadin) Anticoagulant Therapy."

He smiled at me and I nodded. I recognized him, but from where? I knew I had seen him before. But then he looked down at his feet the way people in elevators do, and I could not place him based on the glimpse I'd had of his face.

The doors had almost closed when *ding!* They opened again, as if someone had pushed the button just in time. A family of Somalis — mom, dad, and two toddlers — walked on, followed by that rapscallion among the interns, Elmer Traff, an unusual young man in Buddy Holly glasses who had a reputation for trouble.

When I looked over at where the old doc had been standing, he was gone.

Now, it's conceivable that the old pantaloon was so slight and unobtrusive that he came and went without me noticing, but his disappearance unsettled me. And why would he get on, then off, on the same floor? Had he changed his mind? Or could I have been distracted because I was going over in my mind what I would have to say to get myself in to see Laurel Werling?

On nine, the elevator disgorged me into the secure waiting area outside the psych unit, where I had to wait almost ten minutes, because the nurses' station was empty. All hands on deck out on the floors, I guessed.

Finally an elderly aide showed up, with a name tag that said, BERTA MUELLER, PSYCH TECH. She glanced at my Kingdom Hospital ID and opened the door for me. I confess that I massaged the truth by telling her that I was a "good friend" of Laurel Werling and wanted, if possible, to visit with her and comfort her for a few minutes. I described the spirit rather than the complex letter of our relationship, because there was no time to explain how Laurel and I had shared a horrific trauma, an experience more binding than the circumstances of most ordinary friendships. I just knew that Laurel would be happy to see me and relieved to have the ear of a fellow refugee from the ordeal of Madeline Kruger's demise.

Berta advised me that Ms. Werling was on ward 9D, which she indicated with a nod of her head. She said I would have to wait and ask the charge nurse on evenings, Heather Howe, for permission to visit the patient. Nurse Howe was in a conference room taking report at change of shift.

Would I like a cup of coffee while I waited?

I'd already had tea, so I took a seat on a padded stool and waited. Berta stepped out into ward 9B to help a distressed young man who came to the station looking for a sheet of aluminum foil to protect his head from aliens trying to brainwash him with microwave radiation.

I looked out through the wired glass and

down the hallway marked 9D, where I saw a figure that so startled me I cried out.

Midway down the hallway, in the fluorescent half-light of the interior, I saw the same old doctor I'd just seen on the elevator. The wired glass of the station wasn't the best lens, and the reflected light interfered with my vision, but I was just sure it was him. I pressed my face to the glass and got a better look at him. This time, because of the setting, I recognized him: The "doctor" was the same old geezer who had come to the nurses' station the night of Madeline's death. Mr. Pigs-in-a-Litter himself, the same guy I'd just seen in glasses and a white lab coat on the elevator. Right by the same fire alarm in the same hallway. *In case of fire, break glass.* There he was, still holding the patient brochure he'd had on the elevator, walking calmly toward the station until he saw me. *Do you wanna know what love is?* Then he stopped, turned, knocked on a door, and disappeared from view when he entered that room.

The sight of him threw my heart into palpitations. I tried to stop the panic from spreading through my chest. I took a deep breath and calmly examined myself for symptoms of seizure activity. I had gone all the way off the wretched medications. I felt much better for it, but I had to consider that I might be having some kind of episode again. I wasn't sitting in a chair daydreaming or hearing voices in an aura; I had witnessed an uncanny sequence of events in two different places extending over at least ten or fifteen minutes, not counting what I'd seen two weeks ago! How could an old codger who was walking around wearing a hospital gown, babbling Satanic sentiments about love, and eating pills two weeks ago suddenly be walking the halls in a physician's coat and seeing patients?

I looked for the elderly aide, a nurse, anybody. No joy. Change of shift, and almost everyone in the report room.

I could open the nurses' station door from the inside, but I'd be asking for trouble if I went out onto the ward alone. I looked back down the hallway marked 9D instead. Nothing. The patients were all in their rooms or down in the lounge area, called the dayroom, at the far end of the hall.

All I could think to do was to call Bobby. After all, Bobby had been standing right next to me when the old guy came to the nurses' station that night. I found a telephone on the counter across the way. I went to it, dialed the hospital operator, and asked her to ring the security booth, where I got Otto, who said that Bobby was outside talking (smoking, no doubt!) with Danny and Ollie, the Castleview Rescue EMTs. I left a message telling Bobby to come to the ninth-floor psych unit, ASAP, and hung up.

When I looked up, the hallway out to 9D was still empty, but when I turned to see if the nurses were coming out of the report room yet, I saw an old man in a white coat waiting at the elevators in the secure waiting area. He was holding a satchel in his right hand, with a thick notebook or manual under his left arm. The same old buzzard! Only now he had a black construction-type helmet on; though he was still wearing what looked like the same white lab coat. He turned and looked at me through the chicken-wire glass. The black helmet was embossed with a stylized bug logo and the words *LuvKraft Pest Control.* A patch with the same bug logo and company name was sewn on the left breast of the white coat. The old guy carried an open tool kit with small boxes inside labeled "Rat Attack: Danger! Contains Warfarin. Extremely Toxic."

The light over the elevator lit, the bell dinged, the doors opened. He half turned toward me and I could see the cover on the manual under his arm. It had a skull on it and a steel instrument pointing at the skull. The old one — I swear it was the same old man! — smiled at me and lifted his hat, as if to say adieu, and there was that big white ropy scar switchbacking from his left temple to behind his ear. The same raised livid thing I'd seen on the scalp of the old rawbones the night Madeline had died.

He stepped onto the elevator. "You got some big ones up here," he said, and then the elevator doors closed on him.

Is that what he'd said? It was muffled by the glass, and I'd gotten at least half of it by reading his bloodless lips.

You got some big ones up here?

Into the station came Berta, the elderly aide. I must have sounded like I needed a room out on the floor by the time I finished telling her what I'd seen.

Berta had decades of experience making sense of confused narratives, so she patiently kept trying to organize the particulars while my panic and fear mounted.

"You say you saw a man in a white lab coat. All right, was he a doctor? A respiratory therapist? Doctors do come out on the unit to see their patients."

"No," I said. "I mean, yes. When I saw him on the elevator, he looked like a doctor, yes, and when I saw him out on the ward just now, yes, he wore a doctor's coat. When he left just now, though, he was wearing what looked like the same long white coat, but he also had a helmet and lettering on his coat with the name and logo of the pest control company trucks parked downstairs."

"Did he come through the nurses' station?" asked Berta.

Apparently there was no way to get from the ward to the elevators without coming through the nurses' station. Details, details.

By now the other nurses and psychiatric technicians had come out of the report room. Eventually I persuaded them to let me show them the door and the room the mysterious figure had entered out on ward 9D.

As we walked down the hallway I began shaking with fright. I could barely keep my stories straight, about how I was a "good friend" of Laurel Werling and a volunteer hospice worker on the Kingdom Hospital sunshine ward, because I could not get the old man's face out of my memory. He had been there the night Madeline had died, too. *Do you wanna know what love is?* I was sure I knew him, knew him from before I'd seen him eating pills the night Madeline died. Knew him from my childhood?

We reached the door in the hallway.

No. No. Don't let it be so, I prayed. *Don't let it be so.* Nurse Heather opened the door to what was of course Laurel Werling's room. What we found there was predestined, as if it had happened the first day of creation and had been waiting here ever since in this room on the ninth floor of Kingdom Hospital for us to find it.

Laurel Werling was still in her hospital gown, sitting on the floor, one leg haphazardly folded under her, her neck propped up against a radiator, arms fallen away at her sides.

Every opening and orifice on her head and face streamed an eerie mixture of blood and serous fluid. Even the mucous membranes of her swollen blue tongue and the seam where her lips met the flesh of her face oozed the same pinkish fluid, as if the foul fiend had mixed her blood with water before allowing it to gush out of her in rivulets.

The rest of her body had erupted in dark

140

bruises, where internal hemorrhaging spread outward from her joints like stains under her skin, continuing even as we watched in horror. She looked as if she'd fallen down twenty flights of stairs and then showered in blood and water.

"Code blue!" said Nurse Heather.

INVESTIGATION

An old biddy with a recent head injury and a history of seizure activity doesn't stand a chance against the medical industrial complex and the police states of rural Maine. The Lewiston police department and the head of Kingdom Hospital security investigated the death of Laurel Werling. Unlike Madeline Kruger, who was elderly and nearly dead when she was admitted to the hospital, Laurel Werling was a young woman of thirty-five years, healthy except for a recent acute psychosis.

I was called upon to provide statements to various detectives and investigators, to whom I reiterated the facts as I knew them. I saw an old man in a white lab coat carrying a brochure about managing anticoagulant therapy with the words *warfarin* and *Coumadin* plainly printed on it. Later, I saw the same old man carrying a satchel with packages of rat poison, also emblazoned with warning labels about warfarin. Laurel Werling had indeed ingested warfarin, which as Coumadin is used as an anticoagulant

141

or blood thinner to treat clotting disorders in humans, but is also used as a rodenticide, because in large doses it causes massive hemorrhaging and internal bleeding and deprives the blood of its ability to clot. Humans ingesting warfarin in large amounts die just the way Laurel Werling had died, by bleeding thinned blood from the lips, eyes, mucous membranes, and all orifices, and from massive bruising and internal hemorrhage.

I confess that I downplayed — well, actually, I did not even mention — the part about how the old man I'd seen first on the elevator in a doctor's coat and later in the hallway and waiting for an elevator in an exterminator's uniform was the same old buzzard who'd come to the nurses' station the night Madeline Kruger died. It never came up, and I didn't raise it. Several of the investigators asked in an indirect way about the death of Madeline, and I also refrained from describing the condition of her body or the swarming ants I'd seen that terrible night. I was trying to convince skeptical, rational men that I'd seen the man — or being — who'd murdered Laurel Werling, and part of me knew that I would only hurt myself by including even more fantastic details, real or imagined, that were off the main point. So I omitted them.

A fat lot of good it did me. Nobody believed me anyway. The hospital administrators checked with LuvKraft Pest Control. The company said it had a policy of mandatory retirement at age sixty-five and currently had no pest professionals over age fifty-five. The company had dispatched two teams of rodent control experts to Kingdom Hospital the day of Laurel Werling's death. The oldest exterminator on the two teams was forty-two years old, and the men had worked only deep in the basement areas, near the earthquake damage, where vermin had been reported. The exterminators had at no time visited the upper floors of the hospital or the Kingdom psychiatric ward.

As for mysterious elderly skeletal physicians in white coats, the oldest doctor on staff and present that day at Kingdom Hospital was Dr. Louis Traff, a slightly overweight doctor I knew by sight. After checking with security (Otto) and the hospital operator (Karen), Dr. Massingale reported that no physician over age seventy with hospital privileges had visited the Kingdom that day, and no physician fitting the description I provided had checked in with the hospital operator at any time within Karen's memory.

Everyone was careful not to say it, but the consensus seemed to be that I was either bat-belfry mad, or relapsing and having some kind of a complex partial seizure. Bobby told me that the "ghost" I'd seen was being referred to all over the hospital as Dr. Rattigan, making me the figure of fun du jour.

Instead of admitting that Laurel Werling's

death appeared to be at the very least an unexplained phenomenon, the investigators theorized that Ms. Werling, an experienced psychiatric nurse, had managed to obtain or had stockpiled a supply of Coumadin (warfarin), which as implausible as it may seem, she somehow accessed while being treated for psychiatric illness at Kingdom Hospital. Their working hypothesis was that she had intentionally ingested an overdose of anticoagulants for the purpose of ending her life.

As for the horrid old man, whose face I still see at night when I can't sleep, he must have existed somewhere in my temporal lobe, where like Frankenstein's monster, he'd been brought to life by an electrical storm — only in my case it was a synaptic lightning strike somewhere in the haunted house of my old brain.

Even Bobby sided with the enemy. He'd brought me an African violet several days after poor Laurel's funeral — with a Tilt-a-Whirl of pretty purple blooms — and I was just thinking how dear he could be at times when he said, "Mum, I brought you the violets to get your mind off ghosts."

"That poor woman," I said, and I couldn't keep the tears from spilling onto my cheeks.

"Mum, it's not your fault. She was dotty, so she offed herself."

"No, Bobby. Laurel Werling was not dotty. She was as sane as any other hardworking charge nurse in that hospital. What we saw the night Madeline Kruger died drove Laurel Werling insane, Bobby. If I'm not careful, it will do the same to me."

THE TREATMENT

For years prior, I had been seeing Dr. Lona Massingale, a wonderful person and a no-nonsense neurologist who had treated me for tinnitus and occasional tingling in my extremities. I'd also endured that rite of passage now intimately bound up with the grand climacteric of modern American life — a memory test to detect early Alzheimer's disease. Aced it. At the time, I recall that Dr. Massingale asked me if I'd be interested in trading memories with her.

Dr. Massingale always took time to explain everything and to incorporate my own alternative medicine therapies into any treatment regimen. But after the Dr. Rattigan episode, her careful teaching didn't take the sting out of her diagnosis and prescription. She recommended that I go back on Scyllazine, 100 milligrams twice daily, for apparent continuing seizure activity. To combat what she called apraxia and dysphoria — the unpleasant side effects that made me want to do and be nothing — she also prescribed 100 milligrams twice daily of Charybdisol, essentially the same drug mix Dr. Metzger had recommended in Boston.

If I didn't know better, I would suspect that

these physicians all belonged to a single fraternal secret society and granfalloon, financed by Big Pharma, which allowed them to collude in their practices, diagnoses, and prescriptions. In this global medical conspiracy, second opinions were an illusion on the order of those Wall Street investment firms who issue "research" recommending — what do you know! — the same stocks their investment bankers are selling. One might as well ask another Maoist for a second opinion about the Little Red Book.

I continued seeing Dr. Massingale at the Kingdom Hospital clinic for the next few months. My official diagnosis after my stay in Boston was concussion with contusion and mild hemorrhage in the right temporal lobe, with some nonclinical seizure activity detected by EEG. She had some good news: namely, that I probably wouldn't have to travel to Boston for any follow-up scanning, because Kingdom Hospital had almost finished aggressively expanding its neurology, neurosurgery, and neurosciences departments. New MRI scanning facilities were part of that expansion, and a well-funded recruiting effort was under way to entice a few choice neurospecialists from all over the country to administer and staff the new neurosciences division.

Dr. Massingale warned me that lingering neurological symptoms were the norm for someone my age suffering the aftereffects of head trauma, but she predicted the sequelae would resolve themselves over time. I hadn't by any stretch given in to the medical worldview of my condition, nor had I given up my own investigations into the unexplained (at least to me) deaths of Madeline Kruger and Laurel Werling. But the meds robbed me of my usual energy, and I often found it easy to procrastinate, and even easier to wonder if writing my notes or doing more research were worth the effort.

I assumed that the Krugers had caller ID, because no one ever picked up the phone when I called. I thought about calling from a phone booth at the hospital, but then what would I say when they answered? Aha! Gotcha! According to Bobby, all three of Madeline's children were back in Lewiston to divvy up the spoils of her modest estate, dispose of the house, and split up the proceeds. I wrote two letters — one expressing my condolences and the other asking if Mrs. Kruger had left any papers or memorabilia pertaining to our childhood friendship. The letters went unanswered. Bobby told me that Hilda, the eldest and the executor of Madeline's estate, operated according to the golden rule: Them with the gold makes the rules. And Hilda didn't want Ray or his little sister, Peggy, talking to me about their mother's death or giving me any of their mother's papers.

Whether I had post-concussion symptoms or medication side effects, I saw Dr. Massingale once a month or so for intermittent vertigo, nausea, and difficulty concentrating. I blamed it on the medications, but she said that only time would tell and I had to be patient.

Another bout of vertigo put me on the floor in the kitchen holding on to the refrigerator for dear life and calling for my boy ("Yes, Bobby, dear, it's just like the TV ad, I've fallen and I can't get up!"), the room whirling around me. Back to the doctor I went.

Dr. Massingale and I agreed that vertigo called for bed rest and more tests, or else I might not be so lucky recuperating from the next fall. She admitted me to Kingdom Hospital for a series of scans and more tests. So it was that I was one of the first patients admitted to the newly renovated neurology treatment floor, which was staffed by some of the finest neurologists and neurosurgeons in New England — at least that's what the front-page article in the *Sun Journal* had said.

Dr. Massingale said it was already hard to get a place on the new ward because of the pent-up demand for quality neurological care in the region. And there I was!

Again, I had moments when I was ready to believe the doctors, but what did it matter? I was old and getting older. The medicine sapped me of the vigor I needed to find out what really happened. Without any proof, I was in no position to fight them. I wouldn't be the first person to leave this world with a truth that couldn't be told.

Then I had some visitors.

DR. RAT

Castleview Rescue provides emergency medical transportation services for Androscoggin County. Two of the emergency medical technicians, Danny Odmark and Ollie Svingen, came to visit me in my room and brought me a lovely little balloon bouquet from the gift shop. Nice boys, and Bobby must have tipped them off about how fond I am of stargazer lilies, because Ollie gave me one in a slender bud vase.

I'd met Danny and Ollie several times because Bobby used to work with them in the Kingdom ER, where EMTs spend half their shifts. But Bobby likes a job where the mistakes are fixable and the worries forgettable. Looking after fresh trauma victims and heart attacks in progress was too much stress for him, so he asked for a transfer out of ER. Bobby was punctual, with good attendance, and he passed all the drug tests, so the hospital offered him a job as an orderly providing routine patient transport instead.

Still, Bobby was always hanging out in Otto's security cubicle just off the ER, so we saw a lot of Ollie and Danny. They could be crass at times, because their callings brought them so close to grisly mortality, but their humor was always in self-defense, never malicious. Everybody at the Kingdom loved Ollie and Danny's stories — told in the acronyms and colorful argot of veteran EMTs — in which mythological deities called the Trauma Gods caused most serious accidents and decided who lived and died. Where emergency or accident fiascoes were known as goat rodeos, old people died of TMB (Too Many Birthdays), the rougher class of patients were summed up using a TTR number (Tattoo-to-Tooth Ratio), and motorcycles were known as donor cycles.

Danny carried the balloons and put them on my nightstand. They'd even tucked a card in there — not something men usually remember to do. "Get well, Mrs. D.," was written in Danny's hand if the signatures were any indication, with a loopy "Ollie" added underneath. As usual, Danny appeared to be in charge. Bobby said that when the boys were running hot with a patient on board who was CTD (Circling the Drain) or FTD (Fixing to Die), Danny was usually in the back, running lines and pumping the ambu bag, because his technical skills and medical experience were superior, even excellent for Central Maine. Ollie was the better driver, but also had the "greater cranial air pressure," as Dr. Hook put it, "a pneumo-cephalic" — his way of saying that Ollie was what my long-departed German Jewish grandmother called a luftmensch, an airhead.

Ollie also had a preoccupation, an inordinate fascination — some would say an obsession — with death, especially the eyes of dead people. According to Bobby, he and Otto could be on the radio with Castleview Rescue, and Danny

150

could be describing several FORDs (not cars, but people Found on Road Dead) over the radio: beheaded corpses ejected through wind-shields and impaled on tree limbs, body parts wrapped around camshafts, torsos smeared along the guardrails, brains splattered like bread pudding and road chili on crumpled panel trucks. And Ollie would interrupt with "Yeah, and you should have seen the eyes in that head. One was looking off into the yonder blue, and the other was full of clotted blood and wide open like the last thing that guy saw was Satan serving him damnification papers."

The way Danny told it, if the two of them got let in by the landlady to find a goner sitting up in bed with an unfinished burrito in his fist and the sports page open in his lap, Ollie would go into a kind of trance, set his equipment down, and stare into the old guy's eyes. Danny knew better than to touch the body. If he started cleaning up the corpse or preparing to trans-port, Ollie, without breaking eye contact with the dead guy, would say, "Let him be a minute, Danny." Then Ollie would stare into those eyes, and carefully examine the dead body. As if a fresh corpse was always a spiritual or meta-physical crime scene calling for strict protocol and proper forensic procedures. As if Ollie had to take special precautions, just in case he could still see God or Satan's reflection in the dead person's eyes. Or better, in case Ollie could peer through those glassy black pupils darkly and see the person's last thought before he shed the pelt of life and slipped away into the beyond.

If the body's eyes were closed, Ollie seemed vaguely disappointed, like a pathologist denied an autopsy or a collector deprived of a rare specimen.

Danny said he'd like to open a Roth IRA and put a dollar in it every time Ollie said, "Look at his eyes, Danny."

I thought the boys were just being nice by bringing me flowers, but they closed my door, pulled up chairs, and sat down for a visit.

"Mrs. D.," said Danny, "we wanna talk." He stirred his hand in the space between the three of us, meaning that whatever we discussed should stay right here.

"We heard all about you and the Rat Doctor, Mrs. D.," said Ollie, "and we think the cops and the Kingdom brass disrespected you in the deal."

"Well, I wasn't exactly hailed as a material witness," I said. "Just a foolish old coot with brain damage."

"Mrs. D.," said Danny, "we're just like you. We can't prove nothing, but —" He looked at Ollie.

"What? Tell me, boys."

"Go on, Ol," said Danny. "Tell her."

"Well," said Ollie, "you know there's that Nozz-A-La soda machine right outside the staff room in the west wing corridor on one?"

"Yes," I said.

"It's got a chrome strip running down one side, and housekeeping polishes it so much that I can usually check my hair in there before I drop coins into the slot. Well, I was doing just that the other night, and I was by myself, almost sure of that. And all of the sudden there's a hand on my shoulder."

I could see the skin on Ollie's arm turn to plucked-chicken flesh, and he stammered with emotion, so I knew he wasn't fooling.

"I mention the chrome strip because there wasn't nobody else's reflection in that polished chrome, ma'am. But when I look around, there's an old guy, probably seventy or eighty, with wispy white hair. He's wearing an old brown suit coat and tie and a funny-looking antique shirt collar, and he's got this big black bag with rusty hinges on it. I'm thinking there is something off-kilter about this old coffin-dodger. His lips are almost white, his skin is like paraffin, he's scarecrow skinny and looks more like a mortician than a doctor."

"That's him!" I said.

"Tell her what he said, Ol," said Danny.

"He looks at me and says, 'Can you tell me where they took the children?' "

Ollie shivered. "Brr. I didn't like the look in his eye when he said that, ma'am. So I says, 'I don't work here, but pedes is on seven.' And he looks at me, like, huh? And he says, 'Pedes?' And I'm, like, 'Pediatrics,' and I look down at his cracked old bag — I'm thinking he's a doctor or used to be — and I say, 'That's a real antique, huh?' He looks down at it. Maybe. Maybe not. Then he says, 'Seventh floor, thank you,' and wanders off.

"I turned around and got busy with the soda machine because I don't want to see this guy anymore. I just want him to go away. I can hear his footsteps echoing on the marble down there. I push the Nozz-A-La button. And those footsteps fade away too fast. So I turn around real fast, and the corridor is . . . empty."

"Has anyone else seen him?" I asked. "Has he spoken to anyone else? Has he ever used names? Dates? Is there a security camera in that hallway?"

Ollie and Danny looked at each other.

"I don't think he'll show up on film, Mrs. D.," said Danny. "We'll check with Otto, but if Ollie can't see his reflection in the chrome of the machine, then I'm guessing he don't stick to film either. But the point is, he's *there* somehow."

"He had black caves for eye sockets," said Ollie, "and pupils like two snake heads."

"Were you boys here the night Madeline Kruger died?"

"Were we here!" said Ollie. "We brought her in. She was paws up dead on the kitchen floor, but Danny got her jump-started again."

Danny looked sheepish. "I hate doing that to a Fail-to-Fly who misses the Oregon Express, but when the cops are standing right there and it's in my job description, I gotta do it."

"What's the odds of that one, Danny? You turn on the gas and stick your head in the oven, and five minutes later the gas man from Maine Natural shows up to check the meter. If you put it in a movie, nobody would believe it."

"Did you see the note she left?" I asked.

"Note?"

Ollie looked at Danny. Danny looked at Ollie.

"She didn't leave a note," said Ollie. "Unless the gas man swiped it? No, what for?"

"The cops didn't say nothing about a note, either," said Danny.

"I was told she left a note," I said.

"With everything going on that night, she could have left the Dead Sea scrolls," Danny said, "and we wouldn't have had time to read them."

"Full moon, Friday the thirteenth," said Ollie. "The night that girl from the cath lab died. That's the night it all started."

"What started?" I asked. I knew the boys hadn't been upstairs when I found Madeline's body.

"You name it," said Danny. "That little girl died and it set everything off. The earthquakes. They had a kitchen fire when a jar of grease cracked and a pilot light got it going. Mrs. Kruger was found dead up there. Then you went DFO."

"DFO?" I asked.

"Done Fell Out," said Ollie. "The rats went berserk in the basement."

155

"Bobby didn't tell me about any kitchen fire," I said. "I've got to get back investigating these things."

"You don't have to investigate," said Ollie. "It's happening in plain sight. And it's getting worse."

"Laurel Werling and the Rat Doctor," said Danny.

"And look what happened to Dr. Egas," said Ollie.

"Dr. Egas? That's the doctor who took drugs," I said, "the one who killed the little girl? Bobby told me about that, and I saw it in the paper."

"That's him," said Danny. "Now he's upstairs in the expensive care unit SFJ."

I looked at Ollie.

"Screaming for Jesus."

"That's what I mean, Mrs. D.," said Danny, "everything, including the Rat Doctor, seems to go back to the night the little girl died. That's when the earthquakes started."

"Why is Dr. Egas, er, screaming in the intensive care unit?"

"I'm getting there," said Danny. "The earthquake damaged the fluoroscopy unit in the cardiac cath lab. The same lab where Egas killed the little girl. The vibrations cracked the shielding and the lead casing around the X-ray tube of the fluoroscopy unit. So the next time Egas comes in and turns the thing on to do a heart X-ray, he gets blasted with a maximum unshielded, unfiltered dose of radiation to the tune of six rads per minute for the duration of the procedure, for a total dose of a hundred and twenty rads, and at those levels, *rad* doesn't stand for radiation absorbed dose."

"Nope," said Ollie, "it stands for 'Right about dead.' "

"And listen to this, Mrs. D.," Danny said. He leaned forward and took my hand in his, he was so excited. "The techs, the nurses, the patient, nobody else in that cath lab got fried by that busted cathode ray tube. Just Egas. The mis-fired beam was aimed right at his neck. Right about where his lead apron ended and his coked-up head began."

"Now he's upstairs doing the Chernobyl," said Ollie. "He's got no hair, bleeding internally, AGMI."

I looked at Danny.

"Ain't Gonna Make It."

"Boys, I thank you so much for this. Really I do," I said.

"There's something going on around here," said Ollie.

"Administration is trying to hide it, Mrs. D.," said Danny. "It wasn't right what they did to you. Pretending you were the only one seeing the strangeness going on."

"Danny," I said, "would you please hand me my notebooks? I'm going to make some careful notes and get right back to work on this."

UNLEASHED

Danny and Ollie's visit charged my batteries like nothing else in my otherwise quiet, somewhat pedantic career as an esoteric psychologist. I had confirmation from at least one reasonably objective source that something else was happening at Kingdom Hospital besides my own alleged seizure disorders. Admittedly, the only eyewitness to anything strange was Ollie, the one with the greater cranial air pressure, but Danny seemed to believe him. I got so excited that I did a bad thing — actually a number of bad things. One bad thing can often be rectified or overlooked, but several of them can sometimes coalesce into a compound disaster that sprouts tentacles and develops a self-directed will of its own, the kind of thing my dear old dad used to call a cluster fudge bar.

I had research to do now, and no time or patience for medicated downtime. I didn't have the heart to tell Dr. Massingale, so I went ahead and let them bring me the pills every day, and then I cheeked them and flushed them down the toilet at night. Bad girl. I chased the dregs of the pharmaceuticals from my system with moonlight, sage aromatherapy, and some deep meditation aided by my favorite healing window crystal. I felt energy returning to my tired bones. I was able to take my walks again and go out and explore the hallways of the

Kingdom, using my pendulum to look for disturbances and harmonic convergences.

I phoned the Ladd Library at the Faust campus and ordered copies of the microfiches of the newspaper accounts of the 1939 old hospital fire. It was going to take some doing, they said, but they thought it could be done.

Next, a tactical error. I should have listened to Bobby, but I didn't. Madeline's note, or the absence of it, was troubling me. She must have left it somewhere in the house before committing the final felony upon herself. I couldn't bear not being able to see the note in its entirety. The woman was a writer, for the love of Godfrey, and I could tell by the passages her son, Ray, had copied down that the note was really a carefully formulated, well-written letter: *I will not disturb her peace with cruel remembrance. Sally forgot her scars. My wounds still fester.* I wanted to see the whole document. Here in the hospital, the caller ID on the Krugers' phone would not alert Hilda or anybody else that it was Sally Druse calling, so I held my breath and made the call.

I shouldn't have.

A woman answered, "Hello," in a meek, barely audible voice.

"Hello, this is Eleanor Druse calling, Sally Druse. I was a very good friend of Madeline Kruger. With whom am I speaking?"

"This is Peggy," she said. "Peggy Kruger. I'm Madeline's daughter."

"Hello, Peggy. I don't believe we've met, but I

knew your mother very well when we were little girls, and she tried to reach me the night she . . . passed away. In fact I went to the hospital to see her that night."

"You did?"

Peggy sounded as if maybe she didn't have all her chairs around the table, if you know what I mean. She was agreeable, but clueless about me or any papers left by her mum. As I tried several different tacks to ask after documents, papers, and notes, Peggy let slip that Hilda was in New York for the rest of the week.

"Oh," I said. "Well, is there a chance that *you* could check for any documents or *notes* mentioning Sally Druse or Eleanor Druse? Your mom asked for my help in another note she wrote to me, and I want to be certain I know just what she wanted me to do. Could you maybe just look through her more important papers for any with Sally Druse or Eleanor Druse on them?"

"Sure," said Peggy, but she sounded hollow, like a gourd with the seeds removed. "Sure, I could look through her papers, for anything with Sally in it. Right?"

"Sally Druse," I said, "or Eleanor Druse. I would so much appreciate it."

I left my phone number at the hospital and asked Peggy to let me know right away if she found anything. I could have Bobby hustle right over and pick it up before — well, I didn't say it, but before Hilda got back from New York.

Next I summoned Bobby. Sweetly. I didn't

dress him down for not telling me about the fate of Dr. Egas, or how Ollie had also seen a mysterious old doctor lurking in the corridors of Kingdom Hospital. I could have, but I didn't. Instead, I graciously asked him if he could please check with the Kingdom's medical librarian, Mr. Bates, and see if there were any records or documents predating the fire, news stories about the fire, monographs or histories done about the old hospital on or before the time of the fire. It was a long shot, but I'd met Bates before, he was almost my age, so he probably knew where to find out about the fire, even if he didn't have the goods himself. Anything I could use to unravel Madeline's curious reference to the date of the fire and a girl being lost and not dying in the fire. Even old medical records.

Bobby cut me off with a pained sigh.

"Now that one I happen to know, Mum. They keep medical records for seven years. Ten at the most. After that they burn them, unless they were part of a research study. Plus you're talking about medical records from before the old hospital burned down? That's sixty-four, sixty-five years ago. They don't keep records that long, even if by some miracle the records survived the fire in 1939."

"Never mind medical records, Bobby. How about a list of doctors on staff, doctors who were working here at the time of the fire? There might be a history of the old hospital somewhere. You've got to help me, Bobby."

"I'll try, Mum. I'll go see Mr. Bates. I'll also go rummage around Faust College and see what they drag out of the dustbin over there."

"You tell them I sent you, Bobby. I'm still emeritus there, you know. They took away my office and gave it to some flatlander who teaches statistics, but if anybody gives you any grief you tell them that Eleanor Druse, emeritus professor of esoteric psychology and noetic sciences, sent you."

"Yes, Mum," he said, even though I know for a fact that he couldn't remember my title if it was the last question on St. Peter's judgment day final exam.

ELEVATOR 2, GOING UP

The next day I woke up early and selected my namesake — a druse rainbow crystal — to wear around my neck while I meditated and purged Western pharmaceutical contamination from my kundalini and chakras. Spiritual plumbing, I guess you might call it. I bundled up in my robe, felt refreshed and alert. Mindful, as we introspective types like to say, porous and atremble with the energy fields that govern my little corner of the universe. I set out to take a walk and go visit my old friend Lenny Stillmach, who was upstairs on the sunshine ward with end-stage pancreatic cancer, making ready for his final journey.

I followed an exit sign and took the stairs up

162

one flight to a different floor, where the nurses didn't know me (well, not quite true, *everybody* knows me by now; but on another floor they probably wouldn't question me about traveling alone). Because of my recent episodes of vertigo, I didn't technically have ambulatory privileges, and I had forgotten to ask Dr. Massingale about obtaining permission to go up and see Lenny on my own. I reasonably assumed that I was entitled to a little leeway when it came to rules and restrictions governing ambulation and patient transport. After all, I was practically a Kingdom employee. I knew my way around and knew what to do if I had any bouts of dizziness.

I went to the elevator bank and pushed the Up button. The numbers overhead showed that car 1 was in the lobby. Car 3 was on the roof. And car 2 was three floors down and coming my way. The chime sounded, the doors to car 2 parted, and the same plain old empty elevator car waited: the same faux walnut veneer wainscoting, the same mirrored walls and brushed steel handrails.

I stepped onto the elevator without hesitation and pressed R for the top floor — the roof, which on one side gives out into the sunshine ward, and on the other side once gave out onto an open sundeck. Unfortunately, the open-air deck had been covered with steel mesh enclosures in 1999, because in April of that year one of the Traff boys, Edgar — a first-year surgery resident — threw himself off the roof twelve stories to his death during his second night on call.

Ollie and Danny were in the ER at the time and were able to diagnose Traff's injuries as another Gravity-Assisted Concrete Poisoning, resulting in a sidewalk soufflé. Time of death: three A.M., dark-night-of-the-soul hour. The father, Louis Traff, is still a staff surgeon at KH; he never quite recovered from Edgar's suicide or from the note his son left, which said simply: "I hereby acquiesce to my father's opinion of me." Traff senior glumly took his place in that sad unnatural society of parents who have buried their own children.

Edgar Traff's younger brother, Elmer, is now a medical resident at KH, and I shudder because Elmer's eyes sometimes sparkle with that same deranged energy that shone in his brother's eyes.

The doors closed, and I was alone, on my way to the roof.

I heard the cables hissing and racing through the pulleys, the soft whir of the motor overhead as the car ascended. Suddenly it lurched to a stop so violently I heard the drop panels in the ceiling rattle, and I almost bit my tongue. The fluorescent lights hummed, then crackled and went out, leaving me in total darkness, suspended ten or more floors above the earth in an elevator shaft.

Silence. Then, I heard a feeble cry, so faint I had to hold my breath to hear it, a tiny whispering sound. A child's voice again, but this time I was nowhere near pediatrics. I strained to hear it over the hiss of the cables and the purr of the motors in the neighboring cars. The mechanical noises seemed inordinately harsh and immediate, and when I looked up I saw why: A ceiling panel was ajar, either because repairmen had recently been up there and not closed up afterwards, or because the sudden halting of the car had dislodged the panel and opened a triangular aperture into the dark elevator shaft. I could see steel cables glistening with oil, and shadows scrolling by on the concrete walls as car 1 swooshed by in the adjoining shaft.

The little girl's voice distinguished itself from the echoing noises, and I recognized the same haunting threnody, the same suffering and eternal loneliness I'd heard in my nightmare or seizure or out-of-body journey to the brink of death — whatever had happened to me the night we found Madeline's infested corpse. The child's wordless misery seemed to make that ancient argument against God's existence — namely, that no loving creator would fashion a universe where children suffered. In plaintive, heartrending tones, the voice seemed to ask the unendurably poignant question: *Why must I, an innocent child, suffer so horribly?*

A blast of static made my old heart shudder in my chest.

"Otto in security to elevator two. Are there any passengers in elevator two?"

The fluorescent lights hummed and crackled again, and about half of them struggled back on and relumed the interior with a sickly greenish hue.

Otto's voice squawked from a speaker next to a handset at about knee level.

"Yes, Otto. It's Sally Druse. I was on my way up to the sunshine ward. And, well, I don't know what happened exactly. The elevator just stopped."

"Always two," he muttered. "Always two on the fritz," followed by another burst of static.

"Flip that red reset switch down there near the phone, Sally," said Otto. "That should get it going again."

I found the switch, turned it off, and gave myself a fright when the lights went out again.

"That's it, Sally. Now just flip it back on."

I did. The lights came on and the elevator lurched, swayed, and resumed its ascent.

"That did it, Otto," I said. "It's moving."

"Good."

"Otto, when the elevator stopped I heard a child crying, a little girl. Has anybody else reported hearing a little girl crying in the elevator?"

Long pause, followed by more static.

"No," said Otto, "no reports of little girls crying. I thought I *saw* a little girl on one of the security monitors the other day. But Dr. Hook came down the same hallway right after and said he didn't see a little girl."

I was ready to get excited about this sighting, but then I had a sudden premonition of what would happen if I took my evidence in its present form to the powers that be and tried to convince them that a sensed presence or ghost

166

seemed to be lurking at Kingdom Hospital. They'd examine Otto, who supposedly saw the little girl, and determine that he was legally blind; then they'd examine me, who supposedly heard her, and discover that I was hard of hearing, with a history of tinnitus. Next case.

The elevator continued its ascent, each floor winking in turn along the row of lighted numbers at the top.

I turned and looked into the huge mirror of the car, looked deep into my own old eyes. Seizure? My ancient lights stared back at me. Was the child's voice inside me or outside me?

"Otto," I said, "are you still there?"

"Still here, Mrs. D."

"Otto, when you see Bobby would you tell him that I urgently need a small handheld tape recorder. Nothing fancy. Just a tape recorder I can carry around with me, for dictation and whatnot?"

"Will do, Mrs. D. I'm writing him a note as we speak."

"Thank you, Otto."

LENNY

The sunshine ward was not a place where I would choose to say my good-byes and take my leave, but it was far better than making a pitched battle of it in an intensive care unit. It was called the sunshine ward because it was on

167

the roof with solaria everywhere, but also because it was designed by hospital administrators and psychologists who had no first-hand experience of death or dying — it goes without saying. Only the spiritually tone-deaf would decorate the walls and bulletin boards of a hospice with yellow, have-a-nice-day smiley faces and with motivational posters and slogans featuring cute kittens hanging from clotheslines over HANG IN THERE, BABY, or sweating pitchers of lemonade next to bouquets of flowers over WHEN LIFE HANDS YOU LEMONS, MAKE LEMONADE.

Several renditions of Operation Morning Air stickers (old and new) festooned the doors, windows, computer monitors, and fabric patches in the cubicle dividers. Operation Morning Air, or OMA as its hyper-indoctrinated graduates like to call it, is the newest public relations and corporate wellness and motivational program wrought by Kingdom Hospital's administrator, Dr. Jesse James ("We never make fun of his name," says Bobby). Like all "new" PR and corporate culture policies and strategies, OMA was supposed to wreak important fundamental structural organizational motivational and everything-ational transformations by changing the name of everything, especially job titles. Patients were no longer referred to as patients, or as gorks, gomers, "the liver in bed six," or "the open-heart in bed five," as they had been called in the wards and ICUs in years gone by. Nor were they to be called "revenue bodies," as they were in the executive offices. No. Under Operation Morning Air, patients were to be called "morning air clients."

Only a Dilbert or a Kafka could describe the inanity of Operation Morning Air, and the likes of Dr. Hook and Dr. Massingale found the blithe, pointless optimism of the program to be tedious and demoralizing. The middle managers who pretended to love OMA brainwashed the volunteers and the hourly employees with stickers and slogans until we all walked around like denizens of Camp Happy, smiling and reminding each other to take deep, cleansing breaths of morning air.

Lenny even had an OMA sticker on the back of Casino Queen, a little handheld video blackjack game one of his grandkids had given him. Whenever Lenny was awake, he played Casino Queen with a manic intensity. Beating the thing brought him a rush of ecstasy almost unseemly in a dying person, and losing to it made a storm-swept desolation of his final days.

It was hard for me to prepare him for his journey in such a place. Then again, anybody who insisted on playing Casino Queen as the clock ran out on eighty-three years of life that had taken him through forty some countries and two wars probably didn't much care what the cat posters on the wall said.

It was no chore for me to see the virile young Lenny in the wasted flesh propped up in bed before me. The total self is *all* selves, one for each moment of earthly life, reunited at death.

"Sally," he said, and those blue eyes lit up like a May morning.

"Lenny," I said, and that was all that needed to be said.

Lenny had been a real specimen, Michelangelo's *David* from the neck down, and good old Lenny Stillmach with a big nose and Groucho Marx eyebrows from the chin up. I loved him dearly. We always had fun. We made love only once. Not another soul knew about it, but yes, Lenny and I had been lovers. Our secret. One night only at the height of that heyday of the blood called youth. The big war was over, and the whole country was still celebrating. We had to do it in a chair because Lenny's arm was in a sling. Before he returned stateside, a shell had jammed and exploded, spraying friendly-fire shrapnel all over the deck. There was jump music coming in from the ballroom. It was summer, our blood ran hot, and our hearts were strong. As Lenny liked to say, "It was only the once, Sally, but it was for the ages."

Only the once, and never again. When we chanced to meet afterwards on the peculiar waterways and backwaters of life, he usually had some unsuitable baggage with tinted hair and plucked eyebrows in tow talking about her cat, or I had the insufferably overweening Randall at my side, ever the art history professor, prattling on about the separation of hands in the Ghent Altarpiece, or his latest monograph on the iconography of Hugo van der Goes. At such times, stuck like two rocks in the river of life, Lenny and I used to look across the rushing waters at each other and think: *How did we not end up together? Why are you with that self-absorbed oddball? What is he/she talking about?*

Leonard Stephen Stillmach was born in Sheboygan, Wisconsin, on April 13, 1920. When he got out of high school, the Great Depression still held the country in its grip like a bad hangover. Times were tough, no jobs. He worked two years for the Civilian Conservation Corps as a truck driver and bulldozer and grader operator. In 1940, he joined the U.S. Navy for a six-year tour.

After ten weeks' training at Great Lakes Naval Base, he was assigned to the destroyer USS *Tucker* at Mirror Island, California, and later set sail for Hawaii. On December 7, 1941, Lenny was twenty-one years old and a seaman first class. He manned a deck gun as Japanese torpedo bombers swept down on his ship. He watched comrades die as the USS *Arizona* exploded and sank a hundred yards away.

Later in the war, while on escort duty in the South Pacific, his own ship hit a mine and sank. He was at Okinawa when the war ended.

He saw action again during the Korean War at the 38th parallel just off the Korean coast. He served twenty years in the U.S. Navy before settling again in Lewiston.

I had to laugh at him now. His bushy white head was propped up in bed. His fingers frantically worked the buttons on Casino Queen until the game emitted a series of notes in descending triplets, whereupon he cussed at Casino Queen as if she were a real dealer at the *Scotia Prince* Casino down in Portland, Maine.

Our insane infatuation with each other, our childish enthusiasm for pure fun were never cured by marriage. It was one of those star-crossed calamities of the heart that we did not end up sharing a bed for the fifty years it would have taken us to explore each other's uncharted interiors.

One night only. For the ages.

When the time came, I was going to cover him in rose petals and kiss him. Dear, sweet Lenny.

He set the game aside and closed his eyes. I held his hand and watched him slip into fitful breathing. Part of me wanted to close my eyes for good and go off with him. The other part wondered what Lenny would see when he left his body. Was there a dark passage waiting for him with a pitiful child crying at the top of it? A bestial figure standing guard?

BUSTED

I was reading a lovely passage of Rilke to Lenny about angels: how they don't always know if they are moving among the living or the dead; how if the dangerous archangel took one step down toward us from behind the stars, our heartbeats, rising like thunder, would kill us. It's possible to live a long and fruitful life without poetry. But at the end of our time on earth, everything becomes gigantic. The moments swell and burst the seams of minutes and hours and days. When we are in extremis, words are too big for prose and conversational speech. Only poetry and prayers will do.

For those of us still thrashing about in the hurly-burly predicament called life, it is at tender, introspective moments such as these that one's relations usually barge in with an urgent reminder that interest rates on fixed-rate mortgages are at a twenty-year low, and did you remember to call the loan officer and lock in? In my case, it was Bobby, who intruded on Lenny and me in our little oasis of time without so much as a by-your-leave. He was pushing a wheelchair with two dusty manila folders crosswise on the seat of it and, on top of those, a little handheld tape recorder. Good boy! The folders gave me hope that he'd finally found some helpful research on the hospital fire. I reached for them, but the impertinent scamp swatted my hand away, as if I were a common brat reaching for boiling water on the stove. His own mother!

I shushed him before he even spoke, because I could see by his bug eyes and his quivering lips that he was going to be way too loud. He had the hospital worker's total disregard for the privacy of others. Not just mine and Lenny's — he didn't even glance at the other patients on the ward, all of whom were at life's end, making peace with themselves and their maker, wasting away and suffering, perhaps already communing with the spirits of loved ones. Bobby didn't know and didn't care. He had one thing on his mind: He was angry at me.

"Bobby, I'm reading to Lenny. What is it?"

He parked the wheelchair next to me at Lenny's bedside and began rubbing his scalp the way he does on those rare occasions when he cares enough about something to be distressed or panicked. A one-handed head rub meant trouble; he was using both hands, which meant *big* trouble. The computer must have crashed and taken Warcraft with it.

"Mum, what have you done?"

"I don't know, Bobby. I have a feeling you're about to tell me. Did I turn off the power supply to the computer when I vacuumed?"

"Did you call Peggy Kruger and tell her to go rummaging through her mum's things looking for suicide notes?"

That was easy. I did no such thing.

"Bobby, I simply asked the woman if there were any papers addressed to me or referencing me that Madeline Kruger would want me to have."

Bobby paced and tugged at his uncombed hair with both hands, as if he was thinking about yanking it out by the fistful.

"Mum, Ray's little sister, Peggy Kruger, is a feeb. She's got the mental operating system of a nine-year-old girl. You've gone and set her off, Mum. Ray says Hilda came back from New York and found Peggy banging her head against the floor, sticking herself with forks, crying about some baby that she delivered stillborn at the Kingdom ten years ago. Hilda had hidden a box of papers from her — dark family secrets and such — but Peggy found them because *you* told her to go looking."

Oops. Perhaps I had overreached. Just a little.

"Hilda is on the warpath, Mum. She's talking to lawyers. Peggy's here in the hospital. That's right, the psych unit, and if you go *near* that place, I swear to God, Mum, Hilda will call the police and have your meddling bones arrested and thrown in jail! She's already seeing about a restraining order, because she knows you won't leave her mum's death alone."

I was chagrined, of course, but another part of me blamed Hilda for not giving up the goods weeks ago. Legally I had no right to look at Madeline's suicide note, but morally it seemed unconscionable that the note referenced me and our shared childhoods and yet was being kept from me. Young people these days simply don't respect the wishes of their parents. They arrogate to themselves the right to decide what's best for anybody over sixty-five, as if the elderly are all manifestly incompetent until proven otherwise. Wisdom counts for nothing.

"You just couldn't let it be, Mum," said Bobby. "You had to go and pry. Hilda's here in

Kingdom Hospital right now taking care of Peggy, Mum. And she's looking out for you. You better go back to your room and post a guard. She is a harpy from hell after every hair on your white head, and I can't say I blame her."

"What are those old folders you have there, Bobby?" I asked as sweetly as possible.

"Mum, I want you to tell Mr. Stillmach good-bye and come with me, back to your room."

"If I do, will you tell me what's in those folders?"

Bobby sighed. "Yes, Mum. Now get in," he said, shoving the wheelchair at me.

"Bobby, I don't need a wheelchair."

"I know you don't," he said. Now he was clenching his teeth, fairly snarling at his ailing mum. "But if you are going to hospitalize yourself for dizziness, then the doctors are going to be worried about you falling again and smacking your brainpan on the marble floors. Get in, Mum!"

"Thank you for my tape recorder, Bobby. That's so nice of you to find one for me."

THE PASSAGE REVISITED

I found out later why Bobby was so put out. Having to come fetch me on the sunshine ward was something of a busman's holiday for him. He was off the clock and had been all set to go home, where he'd have the house all to himself for a nice smoke and a game of Bloodfest, when nurse Howe had called down from the psych unit about the Peggy Kruger affair. Bobby had been wheeling a new batch of auto accident victims around all night — a family of four who came in off of an I-495 pileup at half past midnight. Nurse Liz Hinton had kidded Bobby about it when he had to stay and look after me: She'd told him that he was off duty as an orderly, but he was still on call as my son.

I could hear him grumbling just behind my head as he wheeled me in my chair past the nurses' station on the sunshine ward, where I greeted nurse Brick Bannerman, who looked uncommonly frazzled. I later learned that Brick and Liz were both due downstairs in the ER, where it was all hands on deck to receive a new patient, a celebrity artist, Peter Rickman, a first citizen of Maine, who had been struck by a van while walking on route 7 out near Warrington's Inn. Already, whether by accident or design, the major players in the impending drama were coming together at Kingdom Hospital, like metal filings aligned by invisible magnetic fields.

Let me take pains here to point out that I was of sound mind and body. Except for a little dizziness at times and some tingling in my arm, I was completely copacetic: taking no medications, enjoying lots of meditations.

Other than my arm, all systems were normal, and it was an ordinary sunny day at the

Kingdom. I may have been more than cranky with Bobby, but it was in self-defense. He acted as if I'd committed a felony by calling the Kruger household, so I supposed I may have mentioned a few of his shortcomings en route to the elevators: the chewing, his weight, his congenital clumsiness — pick one! — deficiencies of character, habit, and physique that repel all worthwhile feminine companionship, and with them my hopes of ever dandling a grandchild on my poor old rheumatic knees.

He parked my wheelchair in front of the elevator bank by the nurses' station. A chime sounded over elevator 3, a green light went on above it, and the doors began to open. Out of habit and inertia, Bobby was already edging the wheelchair forward. He wasn't paying attention, as usual, and I heard him telling nurse Brick (who was behind the console) that he was taking me back to the neurology ward.

I heard others cry out to warn him, of what I did not know, until I looked ahead through the open elevator doors into a scarred shaft of naked concrete, stained cinder blocks, rusty tie-rods. I knew this place! I had been here before! But where the floor of the elevator car belonged, an abyss opened under my feet. It was as if the skin of the material world had been torn open to reveal bottomless, terrifying, supernatural mysteries plunging away from me in every direction — an open shaft that appeared to drop for miles into the blackness of eternal night.

I felt myself pitch forward in a bout of helpless vertigo, because I knew that shaft. I had seen it almost a year ago while temporarily dead! Near death! December 13, 2002. Full moon Friday the thirteenth!

The elevator car was nowhere to be seen. Stuck up above us being serviced by repairmen, I later learned.

I continued leaning over the dark chasm, because I could not tear my eyes away. I felt Poe's imp of perversity scaling the frets of my spine, his claws charged with electrical impulses that all said, "Jump, Sally!" *There is no passion in nature so demoniacally impatient as that of him who, shuddering upon the edge of a precipice, thus meditates a plunge!*

I seemed poised on the brink of terror and elation, staring again into the hellish chasm I had visited so many months ago as a fantastical hallucination. Here it was again: a vision out of time in broad daylight. I so vividly imagined myself leaping into what appeared to be an eternity of falling that I wondered if I had indeed already taken that reckless plunge. I was afraid to look up, for fear I would rise again in the dark passage, see that fearsome guardian at his watch, hear the voice of that poor girl crying out to me from the realm of perpetual despair.

Before I could summon the courage to lift my eyes, Bobby pulled his mum back from the precipice.

ELEVATOR 2, GOING DOWN

I was trembling from head to foot and craving my notebooks so I could scribble down in graphic detail the revelation that had just opened at my feet. Let the doctors tell me I was beset by some obscure neurochemical imbalance or cerebral contusion, senile dementia or Alzheimer's; I now *knew* different. The elevator shaft I had just seen was *identical* to the one I'd ascended nearly a year before during my near-death flight, right down to the rusty tie-rods and the stained cinder blocks. I wanted to see it again and compare every blemish and detail with the phantasm that came before it. But I was also still seized by the instinctive desire to go back to the safety of the habitual and the predictable: It could just be a coincidence. I should just chalk it up to septuagenarian daffiness. It was just an elevator shaft, nothing more; they are probably all built with stained cinder blocks and rusty tie-rods. In the end, the delicious exhilaration of confronting the unknown overmastered all.

I had stumbled twice into a node of some kind, a passage to the beyond, or at least to the borderlands between this life and the next: what Swedenborg called the First State after death. This vision charged the visible world with a new energy. Everything from the paint on the walls to the floor tiles seemed to vibrate with color and light.

I barely heard the hubbub going on behind me at the nurses' station, where Bobby had summoned the elevator repairmen. The doors weren't supposed to open, obviously, when the cars were not in service. Gee, what could have happened? Like the KH doctors, they were all hopelessly stuck in the flatland world of medical science and engineering, wearing blinders.

Once the powers that be had all the push-pull mechanics of the unspeakably dull sublunary world back in working order, it was time for Bobby to try again. He wheeled me to the elevators and pushed the Down button. We certainly wouldn't be taking elevator 3, seemed to be the consensus view. Cowards. While we waited, I heard Bobby seething and muttering just above and behind my head. Still peeved about the Peggy Kruger affair, still stuck here off the clock dealing with one foozling fiasco after another. Never mind if he almost dumped his wheelchair-bound mum ten floors down an elevator shaft to her death.

I fished my reading glasses out of my robe, put them on, and craned my old head and arthritic neck for a look at the tabs on the folders. All signs still pointed to the night Madeline died, and I had a feeling the folders were at least related to our shared history, but I couldn't see the labels on them because of the way Bobby was carrying them. The chime sounded, the light came on over the second car, and I waited, half expecting the doors to open on the lower half of *The Last Judgment* by Hieronymus Bosch.

Instead, the doors parted and a plain old elevator waited. It was empty, giving us a moment of privacy.

Bobby scowled, felt for something in the empty pocket of his shirt, and groaned.

"Ah, Mum. I brought a letter for you from home. It's from your nurse friend in Boston."

"Claudia?"

"There you go. I brought it in and then I left it in my locker downstairs. I'll bring it up after lunch break."

"Please do. I love hearing from Claudia. Her husband found work in a computer company."

"That so, Mum?"

"It's so. I'm so happy for her. Well?" I said. "Those folders look pretty old."

"They are, Mum," he said. "I can't decide whether to give them to you or not. They have to do with you and Madeline Kruger, and if you call, write, speak to, mention, even so much as *think* about Madeline Kruger or her papers again, Mum, I swear."

"Bobby, I won't. Just give me the folders. What are they?"

Ding! The elevator stopped. I looked up just in time to realize that we were not only in car 2 — the same elevator with the dislodged ceiling panel where, on the way up, I had just heard a child giving voice to the suffering of the damned

— but 9 was lit on the numbers overhead, meaning we were stopping on the ninth-floor Kingdom Hospital psychiatric unit, where I'd seen Dr. Rat and where —

The doors opened, and there stood a middle-aged Teutonic-looking woman, heavyset and big-boned without being fat, like maybe her hobby was weight training, like she belonged in a production of Wagner at the Met wearing a headdress of horns. I recognized the family resemblance immediately. I also couldn't help noticing that Hilda Kruger seemed way out of sorts, verging on outright rage.

She had a swollen, battered old accordion folder that had been stapled, bound with strings, and patched with tape over the years. I couldn't read the labels on the tabs, but I could easily read what was written in black capital letters on the side: DR. GOTTREICH FILES.

Dr. Gottreich. The name numbed me, paralyzed me, like a spinal block administered at the back of my neck; it drove every living thought from my brain. I felt cold, heat, nausea erupt inside me and rush through arteries and nerves to my head, where an explosion of light drowned out the sight, sound, and sense of everything but that name: Gottreich.

Inside I was still feeling my way along that black wall in the dark, and now I realized that all I had to do was push — push once against the black wall — and it would swing open on Dr. Gottreich.

Hilda looked like a butcher about to turn her talents on living human flesh for a change. She shook the accordion file in my face.

"You want the papers, you nosy old bitch!"

Bobby stepped between us immediately and took charge, using a manner and tone of voice I'd never seen or heard from him.

"There's no call for talk like that, Ms. Kruger."

He sounded like a health care professional when he said it, polite but firm. *I'm in charge here, not you,* was his message. I was so proud of him. That's my son and I love him!

Hilda snarled at Bobby and me and shook the file of papers again.

"Everybody who reads these goes insane and tries to commit suicide. You want to join them?"

She threw the accordion jacket past Bobby and into my lap.

"Take them, you old sow. I hope they lock you up in a quiet room with them and give you a razor blade!"

Her face erupted in wrath and she wound up for a roundhouse slap at me.

Bobby stepped in and caught her wrist and started backing her up, off the elevator and out into the hallway, where I saw a nurse and a psych tech watching the exchange from behind the wired glass of the nurses' station. The two folders fell from under Bobby's arm and the papers within them spilled out and splattered, half on the elevator, half in the hallway just outside.

Several sheets skimmed across the floor and landed faceup in front of my feet.

The nurse in the station picked up a phone and punched in a number.

I watched Bobby try to calm Hilda Kruger. I was stunned, still unable to move. I looked dumbly down at the file: DR. GOTTREICH.

The elevator doors started to close. Bobby reached back to catch them, but then Hilda made another lunge after me, and Bobby had to use both hands to stop her. The two of them staggered off the elevator, leaving me alone inside.

The doors closed.

The elevator began its descent.

THE MIRROR BLEEDS TO THE PAST

I looked down at the papers Bobby had spilled at my feet. The closest one was yellowed, warped, stained, but still legible. It was a printed form with ADMITTING in bold across the top. Stamped at an angle, in what many decades ago probably had been red but was now somewhere between brown and rust, it said: DO NOT DESTROY. RESEARCH SUBJECT. DR. GOTTREICH.

Bobby's words from yesterday popped into my head: *They keep medical records for seven years. . . . After that they burn them, unless they are part of a research study.*

My eyes blurred with tears as I stared at that name again. I had to remove my reading glasses and wipe them.

The form itself held the usual particulars of a hospital admission.

Patient Name: Druse, Eleanor S.
Sex: Female
Date of Birth: 11/2/28
Admission Date: 10/24/39
Admitting Diagnosis: Bordetella pertussis, Whooping cough
Primary Physician: E. Gottreich, M.D.
Treatment: Isolation. High wooden partitions around bed. Cool mist humidity. Red clover syrup or tea, expectorant. Broth to guard against marasmus.

I saw more papers, scattered against one wall of the elevator. These had Madeline Kruger's name on them. They too were stamped DO NOT DESTROY. RESEARCH SUBJECT. DR. GOTTREICH in the color of decades-old blood.

The elevator car suddenly lurched to a stop again, so hard my poor teeth rattled in my mouth. I held on to the accordion file in my lap, but I felt papers slithering under my grasp.

An alarm sounded once and cut off, leaving only silence. The lights flickered; then one or two of the fluorescent tubes hummed and struggled back on, casting a gray-green gloaming in the interior of the car.

I looked up and saw the ceiling panel was still ajar, the black triangle still open to the shaft above.

Half the papers had spilled out of the accordion file into my lap. Crumbling old newspaper clippings, medical journal articles, one entitled "Psychosurgical Procedures to Ameliorate Intractable Pain," by E. Gottreich, M.D., Ph.D. More articles from the popular press, even national coverage: "Psychosurgery Cured Me," where Dr. Gottreich's name appeared in a sidebar, and "Wizardry of Psychosurgery Restores Sanity to Fifty Inmates."

Another clipping had the headline "No Worse Than Pulling a Tooth," about procedures that Dr. Gottreich and many other neurologists and psychologists had popularized. "No General Anesthesia or Sterile Field Required for Miracle Psychosurgery." A grainy black-and-white photo of a doctor in a white lab coat, a head mirror swiveled up away from his face. He was leaning over a patient who was awake, surrounded by doctors and nurses in street clothes, and the doctor in the white lab coat held a steel instrument with a handle. "Lewiston's Own Dr. Eb Gottreich, Psychosurgery Pioneer."

My hands shook. I had to settle my elbows on the armrests of the wheelchair to steady them as I peered back through time over sixty-some years and looked into the eyes of Dr. Ebenezer Gottreich.

Death had changed him hardly at all, for he was none other than Dr. Rat and the same old rawbones who'd come for his drugs at the nurses' station. *Do you wanna know what love is?* Why had I forgotten him? Why was he lost to me still?

In the 1939 photo of the Lewiston *Daily Sun*, I recognized the old brick building. Gottreich was posing next to the cornerstone, which read "Gottreich Hospital Built 1870 A.D." This was the place that had burned to the ground in 1939 on the date Madeline had referenced in her note, the hospital where the two of us were treated for whooping cough in 1939. It was called the old Kingdom only because it stood where the new one stood now, but in the old days it was named after the family of physicians who built it in the nineteenth century: the Gottreichs.

Train Sourball Laboratory. Sally Druse, you old crazy coot, why do those words keep —

More newspaper articles, with and without Gottreich photos, including accounts of the 1939 hospital fire. "Two Die in Hospital Fire."

The fluorescent lights flickered again in the stalled car. Silence. Then the little girl's voice, louder than ever before. Distinct. She sounded as if she were on top of the car, crying out to me, trying to reach me across space and time with her pathetic, inarticulate cry, as if she had forgotten words and was forced to plead by intonation only: *Why must I, a blameless child, suffer so horribly?*

Was the child's voice inside or outside me?

The answer was right there in my lap. The tape recorder Bobby had fetched for me. I was trembling so hard that it was a chore to manipulate the thing, but I had my glasses on, and it had a big red button with RECORD printed under it. I pushed it and saw the tiny red light go on and the microcassette's tumblers and wheels turn.

I looked up and through the gap in the ceiling panels, because it sounded for all the world as if she were directly above me in the shaft. Another part of me knew that the voice was unbound by time or space, or worse, that I was hearing the child's voice in the same part of my brain that lights up on the PET scans of schizophrenics who hear God talking to them.

The tape would answer that question. If the piteous voice was real — My skin erupted in chilly gooseflesh. It sounded real, distinctly human, yet not of this world, just as it had seemed in my episode the night Madeline had died.

Which prompted the obvious question: If the voice was not of this world, then with what organs of sense was I hearing it now? I caught my breath and froze as the next consideration loomed: What if I was able to hear this poor spirit's eerie, unearthly lament because . . . I too had passed into the beyond? What if it's true what they say: that death is just the side of life that is turned away from us, and for a short time after the spirit takes its leave, it flits back and forth between the two realms?

What if, instead of just an episode, a seizure, an out-of-body experience — what if this time I'd really flown the coop? If I was just stuck again in a stalled elevator, then why hadn't Otto called me on the radio, the way he'd done before?

I stared straight ahead and listened to the child's voice fill me with terror and loneliness. What if, instead of just teetering on the brink of that open elevator shaft and suffering a reprisal of my near-death or out-of-body experience, I had plunged right down it to my death? Maybe this cozy, familiar, worldly elevator car was the hallucination of a dead woman still clinging to life, a kind of visual rendition of whistling past the graveyard? Swedenborg says that the fear of death is so great and the human psyche so powerful that for an indefinite period of time after death, the souls of the freshly dead project an illusory image of their usual earthly surroundings and friends.

Others say that the dead don't realize their condition until they look in the mirror and realize that they have no reflection.

I held my breath and felt the chill of a fresh corpse radiating out to my extremities. The hair on my flesh horripilated into a hundred thousand antennae, all resounding with the little girl's cries for help.

Had I seen my reflection in the elevator mirror when Bobby wheeled me aboard? I was facing the control panel, of course. Did I dare turn, look into one of the elevator wall mirrors, and learn my fate?

I turned to my right and gazed into the mirror on the wall of the car, half expecting to see nothing but the reflection of the mirror on my left and nothing in between. This is how it ends, a hall of mirrors and no Sally Druse in between, a question mark crushed between two nothings. Instead, there I was. I was never so relieved to see me, warts and all — silvery yellow locks, my mottled hands (I held them up), the faded flesh of my face, age spots, skin tags, hairy moles, and all. Are you a witch now, Sally Druse?

Then, behind my grinning likeness, in the recesses of what should have been just the reflection of wood veneer and brushed steel, I saw a shadow pass, and in its wake — it was as if an unseen hand drew back a diaphanous veil — I seemed to see a darker yet paradoxically more vibrant version of the same confined elevator, as if the fluorescent half-light within the mirror fell on a more luxuriant interior, richly appointed in more extravagant color and detail than the institutional browns and beiges around me.

Behind my hoary image, I heard the child sobbing again in the middle distance. I searched the depths of the mirror first, only because the cries seemed to be located there in space.

The depths of this mirror were darker and far more palpable than the elevator car itself, and shadows seemed to stir in the peripheries, where I saw tongues of fire, a torch? A hallway with a hooded figure carrying a candle? When I turned around to confirm my impression, I was suddenly unable to locate the child's cry in space, because it seemed to be coming from every direction at once.

Then I saw a little girl coming toward me, emerging from the lush shadows in the depths of that mirror. She wore an old cotton johnny, just like the ones we wore in the old hospital. She was pale and thin. She looked sleepless and wasted, like a wraith from *Carnival of Souls*, but I recognized her at once. It was Maddy Kruger right there in the mirror, eight years old, three years younger than me. Her johnny hung on her like a white gunnysack on a scarecrow.

Then I looked down at my own bony, pale little hands and felt my knobby legs sliding inside my own johnny. I was just a skinny little thing, too. We were both living on broth and red clover tea because we couldn't eat. The coughing fits made us vomit.

"Maddy!"

I had forgotten how sick we were. The fevers and the coughing. Why had I forgotten it? Why did I forget all about the hospital? Why was it so easy to remember now? I could see the old hospital right there on the other side of the glass where Maddy was standing. We had the whooping cough, or as we used to call it, the *whopping* cough.

We both heard the little girl crying above us. We looked up and tried to see her. We were in an old wood-paneled, hand-operated elevator, the kind with an inside safety cage and a brass rail and a little man in a uniform who sat on a stool upholstered in red leather and asked you where you wanted to go and said what floor the elevator was stopping on.

The little girl was lost, stuck up there somewhere above us in the elevator shaft. She needed her mommy or somebody to help her.

"Listen, Sally," said Maddy. "It's the little girl again. She's still crying."

"What's her name?" I asked. "Did you find out her name? I don't think she'll answer us until we find out her name."

Somebody must have hurt her. She was so afraid she couldn't use words, she just moaned and cried. Maddy and I tried calling out to her, but she wouldn't answer us with words or tell us where or how to find her. She was too afraid to do anything but hide and cry. Maddy said we would just have to wait until she knew us better and trusted us. Then maybe she would tell us how to help her. But not now. Now she was too hurt and afraid to do anything but cry.

A bell chimed. A tinkling far off in the darkness above the shaft.

"Come on, Sally," said Maddy. "We have to go see Dr. Gottreich."

"No," I cried. "I don't want to go."

Maddy was crying, too. The dark circles around her sunken eyes were wet with tears.

"I don't want to go, either," said Maddy. "But

193

we have to. He's the doctor. You have to see him now. You have to remember him now so you can forget him again. Do you remember what he did to you?"

"No," I said. "No, I don't want to remember."

Maddy took my hand; her fingers felt like bones clutching me.

"It's too late, Sally. You have to see him. You have to remember him so you can forget him again."

I coughed and wrung my gown into a big knot. Maddy started coughing, too.

We held on to each other while a nurse led us through the basement of the old Gottreich Hospital. It was the old hospital, all right, but it looked as if it had been sealed like a tomb and preserved, and we were the first ones to enter it after all of these years. Damp cobwebs and a century's worth of filth clung to the weeping stone walls, which were festooned with lichens, verdigris, and mold. Beards of moss hung from unhinged doors.

Finally we came to a heavy wooden door with a decrepit sign on it that said: PAIN ROOM. That was the nickname for the room. The doctors called it the Pain Room, because inside Dr. Gottreich conducted important experiments on ways to make pain stop hurting.

"Here, you go, Sally," said the nurse. "Maddy and I will be back soon to collect you."

The Pain Room.

Maddy or I said that every time we came here.

We read the sign, saw the word *pain,* and said, "Don't worry, it's just a nickname for the room where they study why things hurt and how to make them feel better."

I remembered that one time, we were almost to the Pain Room, walking along the hallway, just like this, and the lights went out. It was pitch black because we were underground, walking in the old hospital corridor. We had to feel our way along the black wall, looking for an opening, until we found the door to the Pain Room.

Then we pushed it open and could see, because Dr. Gottreich was waiting for us, and he had lit a taper.

GOD'S KINGDOM

THE PAIN ROOM

Dr. Gottreich had a smile made of gray teeth. He wore a head mirror and green pajamas, sometimes with a cloth cap as well. He was old. Older than our grandpas. The hospital, Gottreich Hospital, was named after his dad, who also did important pain research. Dr. Gottreich was almost all the way bald, but was young at heart — sparkling eyes, easy to talk to, and kind, especially to our parents. The moment they were gone, he behaved unlike any other adult we'd ever known.

He talked to us kids the way grown-ups talked to each other. He made fun of other adults, including sometimes our parents, and said things we thought but would never dare say or admit to grown-ups, especially not to a doctor or a minister.

"It's my little Sally Druse," he said. "How are we feeling?"

The Pain Room always smelled of iodophor

196

and camphor and a sweet oily smell — like spoiled fruit mixed with paint thinner — that seemed to cling to the doctor's clothes, the sheets and cloths. It was cold and dank, because it was underground, and the walls were stone.

On the far wall, there were beakers with flames under them, glass flasks, coils of tubing, burners, and glass containers of specimens.

Right next to the door where I came in was a big glass case with a fat canvas hose coiled inside, and mounted next to it was a red axe with a big shiny steel head.

In red and black letters on the glass case it read: IN CASE OF FIRE, BREAK GLASS.

Dr. Gottreich patted the cushion on the examination table.

"Come on. Hop up."

He helped me onto the table and unfastened my johnny in the back so he could listen to my lungs with his stethoscope. It was as cold as a dog's nose. The nurses warmed theirs in their hands first, but not Dr. Gottreich.

"Deep breath," he said. "That's it."

His voice was a friendly purr.

While he listened to my breathing, I looked at posters on the wall just behind him: medical diagrams, drawings of open skulls with parts of the brain labeled, skeletons with the bones all named, exposed eyeballs with all the parts labeled, empty eye sockets with lines and arrows going into the skull at different angles.

"How's the coughing, Sally?" he asked with a kind voice.

"Bad," I said, "sometimes."

"Have you been drinking your red clover tea?"

"Yes," I said.

"Excellent. It's what we call an expectorant. It helps get the bad stuff that makes you cough out of your lungs. Have you been a good girl up on the children's ward?"

"Yes," I said, but I hesitated for just a moment and heard my own voice waver, because one night Maddy and I stayed up late, past lights out, and we got caught playing outside the high wooden partitions around our beds, which were supposed to keep us isolated from the other kids so they wouldn't catch our whooping coughs. The night nurse was angry, so angry that she may have told Dr. Gottreich or written something about it in our charts.

He reached up and turned on a big drum light overhead. It was steel and had large glass bulbs with big hairy glowing wires inside them. Then he opened a black bag with metal clasps on it and rummaged inside.

"Your mommy told me that sometimes you are a bad little girl."

His tone mocked my mother in a backhanded way, as if Dr. Gottreich wouldn't hold it against me if I were a bad little girl because he still had vivid, fond memories of being a bad little boy.

"She seems a little strict, if you ask me," he said. "I told her that a little more fun and some extra candy now and then would be good for your health."

"Oh," I said. "Thanks."

His tools clanked inside the black bag as he rummaged through them looking for the one he wanted. He found a tongue depressor and brought it out.

"Your mommy said that sometimes there are tantrums," he added, with a chuckle. "Sometimes you can't control yourself?"

"She did?" I asked.

"We don't always behave, do we," he said, but then he smiled.

He turned on a bright light next to my head, swiveled his head mirror down, and pressed his eye to the eyepiece. I could see my own distorted reflection in the polished metal as he manipulated the light source. The reflector made a bowl with his eye at its center, as if he were a Cyclops with a metal head. The harsh bright light reflected back from the shimmering concavity. I had to squint because it hurt my eyes.

"Say *ahh*," he said, and stared hard at me with his one beady eye in the metal dish.

I opened my mouth and said "Ahh," but it made me cough and then I couldn't stop.

"Cover your mouth," he said, and handed me a cloth.

I took the cloth, but I didn't use it to cover my mouth, because I saw streaks of blood on it.

"Cover!" he said.

And I did.

When I could get my breath again, I said, "There's blood on the cloth."

"So there is," he said.

He aimed the head reflector and the light again into the back of my throat. I stopped breathing because I was so afraid I was going to cough again. I just stared at his eye and waited.

His voice changed from a warm purr to a probing thing, like one of his instruments.

"I see something I don't like," he said.

He swiveled the head mirror up out of the way and gave me a hard look with his black eyes in his old bald head. I noticed that behind him on the wall was a color drawing of a skull, just about the same size as his skull, with a rubber-gloved hand holding an instrument that looked like a big knitting needle going in the bone above the eye. I couldn't read all of the labels and names on the poster, but there were words across the top in big black letters. The lights shone off the shiny poster right there and made the letters hard to read: TRAIN SOURBALL LABORATORY?

Pretty strange words to see on a poster in a doctor's office. Where were the trains? And was the sourball an acid drop candy or the old sourball doctor in charge of the Pain Laboratory? I tried to get another angle and make the shiny spots go away from the letters so I could read them better.

Then Dr. Gottreich got in the way. I tried not to think about how his whole head looked like a skull, because I was afraid that he might swivel down his mirror again and be able to see right into my thoughts with that beady Cyclops eye.

"What do you see that you don't like?" I asked. "What is it? Am I sick?"

He swiveled the head mirror back down over his eyeball and peered hard at me.

"Not sick," he said. "Just very bad sometimes, right? Like your mommy said?"

I was afraid because with the dish up close to my face and his eye peering through a hole in it, sometimes it seemed like his voice was coming out of a talking eyeball.

I tried to remember when I had been bad. I must have been so bad that my mother didn't have the nerve to discuss it with me. Instead I must have done something that was so bad and shameful that she'd gone straight to the doctor and asked him what could be done about it.

Of course I believed Dr. Gottreich. I could conceive of a wicked man not telling the truth, and of such a man lying to a child for some awful reason. But a doctor? In my child's-eye view of the universe, doctors occupied ranks in a hierarchy somewhere between my parents, Elsa and Pa Bear, and the angels and saints. Doctors were up there with priests and ministers, they belonged to vocations with special powers, and like priests, they were always good and kind to children.

My mother had warned me that there were evil men in the world who might ask me to touch them, or they might try to touch me. She was so stern and cold and dreadful when she talked about it that I felt I had already done something wrong. She told me that if anybody ever tried something wicked like that, I must say no. I should get away from them as soon as possible, because the Devil was in them. "The fiend in his own shape is less hideous than when he rages in the breast of man," she had said. Only my parents and my doctor could touch my private areas.

I imagined that there were many other strict rules about behavior that also didn't apply to doctors. Only doctors could do and say certain things, because they knew all of the secrets about the human mind and body. They took an oath to heal. Only priests and doctors could talk to me the way Gottreich was talking to me, about being good. Or bad.

What did I do? What did my mom say I did that was bad?

I was afraid to ask. What if he named some terrible deed in the harsh light of the examination room that I had forgotten? Something I'd done when I thought I was alone, but my mom had seen it? Or worse, what if he whispered some repulsive secret from one of my nightmares or daydreams, something so vile I had blotted it from my memory? What if Dr. Gottreich knew about some half-formed wicked fancy, a make-believe exploit that I'd contemplated and vividly imagined and enjoyed imagining, even though it never became an actual vile deed? If he named it, I would recognize it. Oh, yes. I'd have to confess that the bad thought was mine, if it had my filthy mental fingerprints all over it, if it was something my bad little girl's imagination had cooked up when I should have been doing chores or my lessons.

What if one of his diagnostic instruments or his specialist practitioner's intuition allowed him to see inside my mind's eye? Shine a light in there, just the way he could shine one into the back of my throat?

"You must not speak to your mother about it," he said.

About what? He hadn't named the bad thing I'd done. Hadn't said what it was that he was seeing that he didn't like. I didn't ask him because I was afraid. Maybe he wasn't saying what it was because it was truly unmentionable and better left unsaid.

"We don't want to upset your mom again. If you have bad thoughts, you must tell me about them. Don't tell the other children about them. You can't talk to them or play with them because you will infect them with your cough. Don't tell your friend, what's her name?"

"Madeline?"

"Don't tell Madeline either. She's a trouble-maker. You don't want to be like her."

"Why? What did I —" I felt about to cry. He sounded so suddenly stern and cold.

Then he saw I was upset, and his voice became a soothing purr again. He patted my head.

"It's okay to be bad sometimes," he said. "Nobody is perfect. God made both good *and* bad, and then He made us so we could choose between them. It's called free will. If He just wanted us to be nothing but good all the time, He wouldn't have given us a choice. Instead, every day is a brand new day. And every day God lets us choose: Should I be good today, or should I be bad?" He chuckled again. "Or maybe some of both today? For a little variety?"

"I don't want to be bad," I said. "Ever."

"I know," he said, "but then sometimes you think very bad thoughts, don't you?"

I saw no point in lying. "Yes," I said.

"God could have just made everyone good, including you and me," he said. "And the world could have been full of nothing but good people and good things."

"Why didn't He do that?"

"Well, I think He knew that it would get pretty boring, right? If everybody was just good all day long and nothing but good things everywhere, then pretty soon good is just same-old, same-old, right? Good here, good there, good everywhere. Good can be so boring. It's just doing what you're told to do. No imagination. No creativity. God wanted things to be — Well, he wanted them to be *interesting*. Like you and me. We're interesting and surprising because sometimes we do things that are good. And sometimes —"

He smiled at me and moistened his lips in a funny way.

"Sometimes you think about terrible things happening to people you don't like, even sometimes your mommy and daddy. Yes?"

Maybe. I couldn't say for sure. I guess he was right.

"These bad thoughts are normal," he continued. "You shouldn't worry about them. But your mommy knows about your bad thoughts, and she's worried about them. So I'll tell her that we have talked. She doesn't have to worry anymore. And you can just tell me about any more bad thoughts you have and we will take care of them. If we have to, we can make them go away for good. Would you like that?"

His head was right next to that colored skull again, the one with the big needle going in its empty eye socket. I tried to read the big black letters at the top again: TRAIN SOURBALL LABORATORY. For just a second I wondered what would happen if the big needle was going right in his mean old eye socket instead of the skull's.

That was probably the kind of bad thought he was talking about. I had sneaked, yes, and done some things I was told not to do. I sneaked and read a book about a bad man who killed an old lady with an axe. My mom told me not to read it, but I sneaked and read it anyway. First, I imagined myself getting killed by somebody chopping me up with an axe, and that was hor-

205

rible and scary. But it was kind of exciting in a strange way, because it was all just pretend. I wasn't really getting chopped up, it was just scary make-believe. Then I imagined what it would be like to chop up an old lady with an axe. And in the story the old lady was mean and stingy. The kind of old lady who would be dead soon anyway. The kind of old lady who was so mean you didn't really mind if somebody chopped her up with an axe. The kind of old lady who got what she deserved.

Did my mom find that book? Is that why she was worried? Were these the thoughts the doctor and my mom were worried about? Other people probably don't even think about being bad, because they are good, of course. They would read two sentences about a bad man coming after an old lady with an axe and then fling the book away in disgust. Maybe I was different. Maybe I had to be stopped before my sick imagination got all riled by reading about axe murderers, before my bad thoughts became bad actions, before I turned into Lizzie Borden.

"I don't want your father to know about them," said Dr. Gottreich.

"No!" I shouted. "Please don't tell Pa Bear!"

"Everything between us is a secret," he said. "We won't tell your mother or your father about your bad thoughts. We'll just fix them and make them go away. Would you like that?"

"Yes," I said. "You can fix them?"

"Yes, I can, my child."

"With a pill? With medicine?"

"With a simple procedure," he said. "It takes only a few minutes."

"Does it hurt? Does it hurt to fix them?"

"Only a little, and then it's all better. Pain is a funny thing," he said. "It only hurts while it's happening, yes? If it hurts just for a second or two and then goes away, it's really not so bad, is it?"

"I don't know," I said. "If it hurts, it's bad."

"And sometimes when there is pain and it goes away, well, that's a new kind of pleasure, yes? Once pain is gone it makes you happy, even if before it came you were just bored. Does that make sense?"

Not really. I started to get down from the table, as if I could make it be time to go just by starting to go.

"Ho, ho. Where are you off to, missy?"

He sat me back up on the table.

"Something else funny about pain. Suppose something really bad or painful happens, but you can't remember it? Then sometimes it's like it never happened."

"If it was bad or if it hurt, I would remember it," I said.

"Not always," he said. "We have medicines, inhalants, that make you forget. And then? Well, it's like it never happened."

"I don't think I want it to happen at all, whether I remember it or not."

"And what if you and I could solve the

problem of pain? Think of that. What if we found out why pain hurts and found a way to stop it from hurting? Think of all the people that would help."

I tried to think about helping people, even though all I wanted was to leave.

"We have to cause some pain to study it, but what if we have medicine that makes it so people don't remember the pain they suffered in the pain experiment? Wouldn't that be nice?"

I started to get down again, but he sat me back up on the examination table.

"Why don't you lie down here on the table and I'll fix those bad thoughts so they don't happen anymore."

"I don't want to," I said. "I think it's going to hurt."

He turned his back to me and busied himself at the table. I heard his instruments clanking. I also saw him pick up a brown bottle and another cloth. He poured something on the cloth and it smelled very sweet and oily.

"It won't hurt," he said. "Pulling a tooth hurts worse than fixing bad thoughts. Even the little bit of hurt, I promise you won't remember it."

I saw him pick up a long sharp thing with a funny handle on the end. He saw me looking at it, so he palmed it in his big bony hand, set it down in front of him, and covered it with a pale green cloth.

I saw the drawing of the empty skull again on

the wall with the big needle aimed above it into the bone above the eye. It wasn't a knitting needle. I could see the drawing now because the light of his head mirror wasn't blinding me anymore. The big knitting needle looked like an ice pick, and that's just what I had seen his bony hand cover with the green cloth.

His voice purred again. The soft sweet voice he used when he talked to our parents.

"Lie down, Sally."

I didn't want to lie down, but he held me behind the neck with his claw hand and made me.

I looked at that skull drawing again, the gloved hand, the ice pick. With my head lying on the table, I had a new angle on the poster; the shine was all gone from the big black letters. I could read them now, but I didn't know what they meant: TRANSORBITAL LOBOTOMY.

I started to cry and cough, and then I realized that there was somebody else crying in the Pain Room with me. Another little girl. At first I thought it was Maddy Kruger, but it wasn't. This little girl was white as a bone and her grimy old johnny hung on her like calico rags. She had a bell tied around her neck on a piece of silk, and she was ringing it. I could see right through her to the beakers boiling right behind her. She was half not there. She was crying even louder than me. She had black circles around her eyes like Madeline's. She was clutching a dolly and crying.

I don't think Dr. Gottreich could see her. He

was busy laying his instruments out for whatever he was planning to do.

I saw the sharp instrument again. It looked more like a wood- or metal-working tool, not something a doctor would use on a person or a little girl. Why was an ice pick in a doctor's tool bag?

"I don't want to fix my bad thoughts anymore. I just want to go back to the ward."

"Do you hate your mommy?" he asked me. His eyes were black and cold. "Do you hate her? Do you want to hurt her? Is that why you don't want to fix your bad thoughts and keep them from happening again?"

"No," I cried. "I don't hate my mommy. I love my mommy!"

"Love?" He laughed harshly. "Do you wanna know what love is?"

I started coughing and I could not stop. *Whoop, whoop, whoop.*

He poured more fluid from the brown bottle onto the rag. Sweet oily fluid.

Whoop, whoop. I could not stop. I couldn't breathe.

"Cover," he said, and handed me the cloth.

"Cover," he said, and pressed the rag against my nose and mouth.

It smelled like turpentine, and just the one breath made me woozy. I closed my eyes to stop the room spinning. I felt him pull open my left eyelid. I saw him holding that instrument, holding it just like the rubber-gloved hand in the drawing on the wall. Aiming it at me. I felt pressure above my left eye, a tap. A blow. A red explosion inside my head. I pushed him away. The sweet smell made me dizzy.

The girl with the bell started screaming, and her tears streamed out of her eyes in black rivulets, as if she were crying black ink or venous blood. She screamed so loud I felt the vibrations in the examination table. The hard mattress under me started shuddering and bouncing. Then I saw that the walls and cabinets were shaking and bottles and jars and instruments were falling off the shelves and shattering.

An earthquake.

The little girl walked toward the door, and she waved for me to follow her. She was still screaming, and it seemed for all the world that her screams reverberated in the foundations of the place and caused the earthquakes.

She waved at me again. Hurry!

I hopped down from the table, ducked under Gottreich's arm, and ran to the door. When I looked back, the whole room was shaking and cracks appeared under our feet in the cement floor.

"Wait!" said Dr. Gottreich. "You will return to the procedure table *now*, young lady!"

He staggered toward us, still holding that sharp thing in his hand.

Against the far wall, I saw the gas jets under the boiling beakers and the lab equipment. The tubing to the gas burner ruptured and the flame

211

got brighter, rubber blistering, hissing, and dribbling over the lip of the table. The flames spread along the tubing and tabletop and caught a box of glassware on fire, which instantly went up in flames.

I turned to run, but then I saw the glass case with the hose spooled inside of it. IN CASE OF FIRE, BREAK GLASS. And next to it —

I grabbed the red axe with the big shiny sharp head. I swung it back over my shoulder to smash the glass with it. IN CASE OF FIRE . . . Then a bony claw-hand gripped my other shoulder and spun me around, hard.

It was Gottreich. His face was a snarly mess of rage. He looked like he was going to blame the fire on me.

He held the ice pick in his hand, and it was tipped with blood. My blood. He planted his foot to lunge at me, but right then the little girl rang her bell. She was standing off to my left, and with her was a monster, a creature the likes of which I had never seen — a jackal, a giant anteater? — but it stood on two legs like a man. Its eyes seemed human, but its teeth flashed like white razors. It was a hideously fearsome-looking thing, but it behaved like the girl's pet.

I don't think Gottreich could see them, but I know he heard the bell, because he was almost on me when he suddenly looked toward them and the sound of the ringing bell.

Too bad for him.

I saw his white-knuckled fist close around the

handle of that bloody ice pick; the sweet stink of that turpentine stuff he'd pushed in my face still made me unsteady and thickheaded. Gottreich looked back at me one second too late. I didn't have time to think, I just swung for the fence. Ask any of the boys at the South Lewiston Little League, major softball division, Sally Druse can hit when she has to, and that's just the way it felt. I aimed for the side of his head, because I didn't want that ice pick poked at my eyeball ever again. I saw the axe blade reflected in his head mirror, then shut my eyes so I wouldn't see it hit. I heard it instead, a sound like my mom dropping a melon on the flagstones in the kitchen.

When I opened my eyes, the old buzzard was down, and the fire was spreading along the tabletop, more boxes, cloths, and stacks of papers combusting as the fire crawled along them like a living thing.

The creature leaned forward on its furry legs and claws and poked its snout around the caved-in hole I'd made in Gottreich's head, sniffing the wound like a dog appraising tainted meat.

I wiped my left eye and my fingers came back with trickles of blood on them. I looked down at Gottreich's stoved-in skull.

"Pain only hurts while it's happening," I said. "If it hurts just for a second or two and then goes away, it's really not so bad, is it, Dr. Gottreich?"

The bottle of brown fluid that Gottreich had used to soak the cloth had spilled, and the liquid had made a tongue-shaped puddle on the floor that almost reached to the fire.

I looked for the little girl. She was still ringing her bell. Louder. She stood at the door to the Pain Room and waved me toward her again. Hurry!

I ran out the door and into the hallway.

Boom! A flash, and the heavy wooden door banged open and splintered.

An explosion. I ran down the hallway and looked for the stairwell to get out of there.

The little girl was gone. I couldn't see her, but I could hear her bell ringing. Always just ahead of me, leading me down the hallway and up the stairs to the main floor.

An old nurse in a gray uniform, white nylon stockings, and a white nurse's cap was coming down the stairs to the laundry room. She watched me running up to her.

She heard the bell ringing, too. She smelled the smoke.

"Fire!" I cried.

RISEN

Chimes ringing. Electronic beeps. Radio static. A woman's voice.

"Is that normal sinus rhythm?" she asked.

"I got rhythm," a man sang, and I recognized

the voice. It was Bobby's friend, Danny Odmark, the nice EMT from Castleview Rescue.

"I got music," said another voice. It was Ollie! Danny's partner. What were those two goofballs doing bending over me in the elevator?

The boys were sure being silly. A lot of people were huddled around and staring down at me. Somehow I'd gone from the wheelchair to the floor, as in flat on my ancient back and staring up at the ceiling.

"I got my gal," sang Danny. "Who could ask for anything more? I've got daisies in green pastures . . ."

"I've got my gal," Ollie sang. "Who could ask for anything more?"

"There was a fire," I said. "I was yelling fire, wasn't I?"

A good-looking young man in a white coat leaned over me and listened to my lungs with a stethoscope. It was Dr. Hook. I recognized him. He had never worked on me per se, so this was my first close look at him. What a handsome devil. The scuttlebutt around the hospital was that he and another doctor, Christine Draper, were sweet on each other.

"The first amendment does not give you the right to cry 'Fire!' in a crowded elevator," said Dr. Hook.

Well, they all thought that was pretty funny, and I have to admit I did, too, even though I didn't quite have my bearings yet.

"What happened?" I asked. "If I may be so bold."

"There was another one of those shakers, Mrs. D.," said Danny. "Not a bad one, mind you, but enough to make the elevators kick off. Once they came back online, Ollie and I were going to the roof to watch the winter storm coming in. And there you were. AGA."

I looked at Ollie.

"Acute Gravity Attack."

"You're breathing and you got a pulse, Mrs. D.," said Danny, "so you don't need us."

"I think you just went DFO again," said Ollie.

"Done Fell Out," I said. "Right?"

"There you go, Mrs. D.," said Danny. "You'll get your EMT certification before too long."

I smiled at them. Such nice boys.

I could see the fluorescent tubes all lit up above their heads. Somebody had all of them working again.

Medical equipment and sterile packaging, and beeping monitors were strewn all around me — all at the ready, but fortunately not needed this time. More chimes, coming from the equipment, I guess. But I also heard a bell ringing, or the echo of a bell ringing.

A mask covered my nose and mouth, and air, or oxygen, I guess, rushed against my face and sounded like the roar of thunder . . . or flames.

"You're gonna be all right, Mrs. Druse," said Dr. Hook.

Danny hurried around to the foot of the

216

gurney I'd been placed on, and Ollie took the head.

Then I heard them both count, "Mississippi one. Mississippi two. Mississippi three!" and I was hoisted aloft and hauled out of the elevator.

"Wait!" I said. "My papers! The files!"

"I got them, Mum."

"Bobby! Is that you?"

He was just outside the elevator, waiting to see if his dear old mum was okay.

"I got all the papers," he said wearily.

"Good boy, Bobby! And the tape recorder. Where's the tape recorder?"

"I got that, too, Mum," he said. "I got it all right here."

"I'm so proud of my best boy," I said. "I love you, Bobby."

"I love you, too. You had the tape recorder pressed right up against your ear, Mum. Were you trying to listen to it?"

"I don't remember, Bobby. I'm sorry. Bobby, keep those papers safe for me."

"I'll put them in my locker, Mum. They'll be safe."

God had blessed me with the finest son, a comfort in my old age, the anchor of my life.

MEDICAL SUPERSTITIONS

POST-DFO

All I wanted to do was go back to my room and study the papers Hilda Kruger had thrown at me on the elevator. I wanted to read all about that nasty old Gottreich and the fire; see if I could determine what he'd done to poor Madeline, God rest her soul. As my memory of the unspeakable, unthinkable events had been restored, it was clear that in my case the beast had only made a partial attempt at one side of my brain, had clearly not severed the white fibers that connect my left frontal lobe to the rest of me, and instead had inflicted only the minor scar that the doctors had seen on my scan images in Boston. It could have been much worse for poor Madeline. I had no way of knowing unless she left papers relating to the brutal procedure and her experiences at the hands of that diabolical man. Worst of all, it was apparent that here at the Kingdom, the borderlands between life and death were inhabited not just by the lost soul of a nameless innocent, but also by Evil itself. Dr. Rat could strike again at any time. I put on my druse crystal and my crucifix for protection. I'd killed him before (and scarred him for eternity, from the looks of that livid zigzag decorating the left side of his spectral skull), and if need be I would kill him again using any weapon, natural or supernatural, that came to hand.

Madeline knew that I'd repressed it all, blocked and blackened over the nightmare of Gottreich and his Pain Room. "God has blessed Sally Druse with a memory more merciful than mine. I will not disturb her peace with cruel remembrance."

And God bless you, too, Maddy Kruger. Clearly she intended to leave this world without ever disturbing my peace with cruel remembrance. She tried to rush into the secret house of death and failed. When she woke up at Kingdom Hospital, built on the site where Evil touched us, where she had received her "still festering wounds" . . . what happened then? She must have seen the little girl before the beast did his work with the ice pick. Yes, and that's why she wrote me that urgent note: "The little girl is back among the lair of the living. She needs our help." Until Madeline saw the little girl there that night, she must have believed that the child had perished in the fire: "The fire did not kill her." But the little girl I saw in the Pain Room was insubstantial, a presence, not flesh and blood. How would a ghost die in a fire? Maybe

Madeline didn't know the little girl was a ghost? Maybe Maddy had just heard her cries? Had not seen her presence or felt her screams reverberate in the very stones of the foundation, the way I had.

There was an earthquake the night Madeline died, too! Maybe the little girl's screams made another earthquake that full moon Friday in December of 2002. Maybe she tried to save someone else by —

The ringing bell! The Lewiston *Sun Journal* article: "Ringing Hospital Bell Blamed On Malfunctioning Elevator Chimes."

Maybe the little girl had tried to save Madeline? Or someone else? I thought back to the many disturbances of that Friday. What about the little girl who died that night? The heart patient, who died because of the cardiologist? Egas. The coke-head cardiologist. The *Sun Journal* article had a photo of her — and him! — the one Bobby had told me about, Theresa Bradley, and he said that she had died from a botched procedure. Had the ghost girl tried to save Theresa? Is it the suffering of innocents that disturbs the ghost girl's rest? *Why must I, an innocent child, suffer so horribly?* Those were the words that I'd imagined I had heard in her inarticulate misery. Was it the suffering of the innocents at the Kingdom, her own suffering, or the suffering of other children in the name of medical research or scientific progress? Is that what inspired her fear and confusion, caused her to lose her way between life and death, and brought her back to the lair of the living whenever it happened again?

All questions that had to wait. Why? Because medical science owns us body and soul and holds our poor, frightened age in its fearsome sway. There was no time for researching matters of the spirit just yet, because armies of people in white lab coats wanted to know what my hemoglobin count was, my creatinine levels, the partial pressure of oxygen in my blood, and my pH. First, a battery of flatlander tests had to be conducted to determine what had happened to me in elevator 2. If I voiced any objection, I was given to understand that I would be summarily discharged and sent home.

No expensive care unit on this go-round, but Dr. Massingale examined me thoroughly, had my precious bodily fluids drawn and analyzed. She sent me up to the brand spanking new MRI facility, where the tech slid me into another big beige hair dryer and scanned me.

The manufacturers of these devices know that human beings in mortal fear of their lives are going to have their heads stuck in here for twenty minutes at a time, waiting to have their medical destinies revealed. So why not inscribe something inspiring or comforting on the casing of the device, instead of SERIAL NO. 4D617279204A656E73656E?

After that, the techs came in and put electrodes and paste all over the old brain box for another EEG. Cranial checks. Not once, not twice, three times, by three different doctors.

Finally I made it back to my room, only to find Dr. Massingale there and impatiently waiting. She seemed less friendly — dare I say put out? She said that the results of all the testing would take several days to assemble and digest, but that after she had all of her data, she was planning what she called "a Sally Druse summit." I could tell she was convinced that I'd had another seizure, which to her way of thinking had happened only because I'd stopped taking my medications. As soon as she established that, she was going to lay down the law and tell me that if I was not going to cooperate with my treatment, I would be discharged and sent home.

Just as I was thinking that I really wouldn't mind going home, she also mentioned in passing that Hilda Kruger had seen to it that my privileges as a Kingdom Hospital volunteer had been revoked. I was no longer a volunteer, no longer permitted on the sunshine ward or anywhere else I had no business being as a patient, and I would not be allowed to visit anyone in the hospital without explicit permission from the patient and the attending physician of the patient.

All I could think of were Madeline's words in the note she'd written to me that night. Probably the last words she'd written in her life: "The little girl who saved us is still lost. She needs our help. Come see me."

This was a fine predicament. To continue my

investigation of the poor child's sensed presence (whose existence was as real to me as the floor beneath my feet) I was going to have to play sick and pretend I was having seizures to keep the medical materialists happy. Otherwise the esteemed physicians of Kingdom Hospital would discharge me and not let me back in the hospital to help the poor child find rest.

Dr. Massingale, typically a woman of almost infinite patience, had apparently exhausted her tolerance when it came to my not taking my medicine.

"If you aren't going to accept treatments or take the medications we prescribe for you, then there's really no reason for you to be here, is there?"

I'd have to do my very best to contact the child's spirit within the time remaining before Dr. Massingale got my test results. I was certain those would prove to them once and for all that my brain was as right as rain, and then they'd send me home and not let me back in the front door without explicit permission. A catastrophe, and not just for the child's restless spirit. At my age, I usually have at least one close friend who is in extremis and dying, and I naturally wanted to be near them, especially dear Lenny. Surely I could get in to see him?

I had a thousand questions about Madeline, the fire, the evil Gottreich, the little girl's sensed presence, the creature who seemed to be the little girl's familiar or pet, but I was sore all over, my joints throbbing, my old bones and brain cells wearied by my journey back to the place where Evil touched us.

The only craving left in my empty head was for the death of each day's life, mother night, sister sleep.

BOBBY

The morning brought a respite from the lab tech vampires and medical technicians and the prying rays of scanning devices, but who knew how long it would last? Before long, some ambitious young physician (with a new family and medical school loans due and owing) would notice that I wasn't having any billable procedures performed upon me, whereupon more tests would be ordered.

I summoned Bobby because I wanted to review the documents Hilda Kruger had thrown at me, and I wanted to find out what, if anything, his trip to the Ladd Library at Faust College had turned up.

He came in fresh off the night shift, in the usual pother of scrambled biorhythms, aggravated by sleeplessness, sugar, and nicotine.

He sat down and rubbed his head with his right hand. Then his left joined in, and I became concerned.

"Mum, this is the end."

"Don't say it, Bobby."

"Don't say what?"

"You're not going to run away from home again, are you, Bobby?"

"Mum, this nonsense must stop. Even the doctors all say it has to stop."

"What has to stop?"

I tried to look innocent, but he wasn't taken in. Instead he gave me the hardest look I'd seen, well, probably since I burned all of the girlie magazines I'd found under his bed.

"The world is full of wonders, Bobby. Let's not spoil it by bickering."

"It's not bickering, Mum. It just has to stop. I work at the Kingdom, and you are becoming a threat to my continued employment."

"Nonsense, Bobby, I —"

"And this research of yours is a threat to your health. The doctors told me I should throw away all of those papers of yours so that you'd stop getting all riled up about Madeline Kruger, about who died in the fire, about voices in the elevator, and such." He rolled one fearful eye my way. "So that's what I did. I got rid of them."

He closed his eyes and started in on another two-handed rub.

"Bobby, you didn't throw away those papers, did you?"

"That was a good hunch about those old records, Mum. Those old records were stored below ground in fireproof rooms, even in the old hospital. Some of them survived the hospital fire, and the research papers obviously got kept.

Those Gottreichs apparently were famous for a while there doing pain research, but then I guess nothing came of it. But the records got kept."

"Yes, they did, Bobby. You didn't answer my question."

No eye contact.

"Mum, I took the folders back to medical records, and I gave all of those other papers back to Hilda Kruger. I told the doctors that's what I was planning to do, and they said it was probably a good plan, given the way you've been behaving."

Still not even a glance from him.

"Bobby?"

Now he managed just a sideways glance, a furtive one, before he went off into another head rub.

"I see the way it is."

"You do?"

"I do," I said.

"And you're not angry?" He brightened at the prospect, but only for a moment.

"I'm not angry, because the papers are still in your locker and you were testing me to see how angry I would get if you actually had given them back to Hilda Kruger. The answer is *very angry,* Bobby. Now please go get me those files. Now!"

He groaned so loud it made the sputum cup reverberate on my nightstand. If he had had three hands, he'd be doing a three-handed rub.

Finally he staggered to his feet and shambled off to get me the papers.

"And the tape, Bobby. I need the tape that I made!"

"There's nothing on it, Mum. I already listened to it."

"I need the tape," I patiently repeated. "There's nothing *you* can hear on it. I've always sensed that whatever frequency the little girl operates on is not within bandwidths normally heard by the ungifted. If that were the case, everybody riding in elevator two would be filing nightly incident reports in Otto's office about children crying."

"Yes, Mum."

THE SENSED PRESENCE

Dr. Massingale was making it difficult for me to remain in charge of my own care. It was, of course, out of the question for me to tell her what I knew about the little ghost girl, about Madeline Kruger, about Gottreich's crypt of horrors called the Pain Room. I'm sure she would thrill to my descriptions of a giant anteater nuzzling the brains of a Nazi lobotomist, but I was not gullible or naive enough to turn over that kind of ammunition to a physician. She was a nice woman, but she was also part of a raiding party from the flatlands of science. At this stage of my life, they were coming into formation on the high ground around me, looking down on me for any evidence of my mental incompetence, which — if it could be proven to a reasonable degree of medical certainty — would give them what they really wanted: control of my medical care.

Even if I could win Dr. Massingale's trust and confidence, I would be unable to convince her that I had traveled in the land between life and death. It would be easier to describe a Mozart concerto to a profoundly deaf person. Instead, I wisely told her only what I hoped would cause her to order tests, the results of which would help me prove my case.

She was already hellbent on ordering any test likely to show that I had experienced another seizure. (Note that even Stegman and his Boston cronies didn't actually witness me having any seizures; they had merely interpreted EEG results, which seemed to suggest that I had experienced nonclinical seizures.)

First and foremost, Lona Massingale was a medical scientist, so to win back her trust, I would have to use the old 52-card deck to play her game — science — and systematically approach the phenomenon of the voice and the sensed presence of the little girl. To do that, I needed other tests to be ordered.

Brain scans of schizophrenics show that auditory hallucinations are "heard" or processed in different parts of the brain than real voices. If only I could be scanned while riding in elevator 2. If I could signal the technicians and alert them to snap the photo of my gray matter right when I was hearing the little girl's voice, a functional brain image could show whether the voice came from within or without.

Right, and if my uncle were a woman, he'd be my aunt.

I am enough of a scientist to realize that the problem of the little girl's voice presented several possibilities, some of which I could explain to Dr. Massingale, some I would take to the grave with me. For instance, it could be that I heard the voice directly in some precognitive or clairaudient portion of my brain, because the little girl somehow had direct access to my neural circuitry. Maybe when I heard it, I used the same part of my brain that is active when mystics peer into eternity. Yes. And so what? Medical science would be unimpressed, and I would be diagnosed as having auditory hallucinations, even if they could watch pictures of them on a scan.

How to convince Dr. Massingale that the voice was not an auditory hallucination? A flatlander would ask: Was I really hearing a voice? Or hearing something else? So I needed a hearing test to rule out tinnitus. If the tests were negative for tinnitus, then that would be *some* evidence, at least, that the anguished cries I'd heard so vividly in elevator 2 and on the night Madeline died were not simple ringing in the ears.

Next, I needed a sound professional to examine the tape I'd made. If I could get Dr. Massingale to at least entertain the possibility that my "episodes" consisted of something more than seizures, then the question remained: Was the voice of the little girl a "real" acoustic phenomenon? Could a confused and frightened spirit trapped between life and death somehow generate sound? Perhaps her cries were actual noise, but inaudible to the human ear. Only professional audiologists and sound technicians could answer these questions, and Dr. Massingale was my best bet for getting those tests ordered, certainly with regard to having my own hearing tested.

Give her credit, she played along and ordered the tests I'd wanted done as well, probably because they were covered by insurance. She also agreed that we should systematically approach the phenomenon of the voice. The tape was sent to a sound technician and I was sent upstairs to an audiologist and otologist, Dr. Marcia Limen, who put me in a sound booth with the old earmuffs on and beeped at me for half an hour or so.

Of course I was eager to know the results right then and there, but I was told by an icy Dr. Limen that I would receive the results of the tests and whatever mysteries had been revealed in the sound booth from my primary physician, Dr. Massingale, presumably at the impending Sally Druse summit.

TRAIN SOURBALL LABORATORY

I returned to my room, where I was to await

the verdict of the medical industrial complex and its prolix testing. Who pays these bills, anyway? The students at Faust College? The taxpayers? The insurance companies? Who was getting billed for the insatiable lust of these medical scientists to test every molecule in my body and examine it for signs of seizures?

It's a riddle I assume will be answered long after I'm dead. I'll leave explicit instructions to Bobby in my will not to pay them. To skip town if he must.

Meanwhile, I seized the day to catch up on my studies. Bobby had left the file on my nightstand. I rummaged through it and found the newspaper articles that had fallen onto my lap in the elevator.

"Two Die in Hospital Fire," said the headline of the old *Daily Sun*, November 3, 1939, reporting on the fire that occurred on All Souls' Day, November 2. Caused by an ether explosion in a basement laboratory. The story told how the renowned Dr. Ebenezer Gottreich, named after his uncle who owned and operated the Gates Falls Textile Mill on the very same site during the Civil War, had perished in the fire, along with one of his research subjects, a juvenile delinquent, Paul Morlock, age fifteen. The Morlock boy had been under Dr. Gottreich's care for violent antisocial behaviors. He had apparently been receiving sensory deprivation therapy in the hope of curtailing his aggressive impulses and at the time of the fire had been submerged in a saline tank in a room adjoining the laboratory where Dr. Gottreich was working. Dr. Gottreich and his patient were unable to escape.

All the other patients and staff were able to evacuate the hospital well before the fire got out of control, because they had been alerted to the outbreak of fire by loudly ringing bells and a child crying.

The article, and the ensuing coverage in the other clippings Madeline had collected, went on to note that this was the second fire to have occurred on the site. In 1869, on November second, exactly seventy years to the day, the Gates Falls Mill, owned by Ebenezer Gottreich's uncle and namesake, had burned to the ground.

Two fires! This *was* news to me. We'd all grown up knowing the old Kingdom had burned, but I had never so much as heard about the mill. A sidebar story on the original Gates Falls Mill fire told how the mill had employed two hundred textile workers making uniforms for Yankee soldiers during the Civil War. When the mill burned in 1869, most of the adult workers got out in time. But the child laborers — mostly Irish immigrants — worked on the lower levels underground, where they tended the dyeing and bleaching vats and worked twelve-hour shifts during peacetime. Most of the children did not get out.

This was fuel for thought, and I dug out the

note Madeline had written me the night she'd died in the hospital.

DEAR SALLY: THE LITTLE GIRL WHO SAVED US IS STILL LOST. SHE IS BACK AMONG THE LAIR OF THE LIVING. THE FIRE DID NOT KILL HER. SHE NEEDS OUR HELP. COME SEE ME.

Which posed a new question: *Which* fire did not kill the little girl?

In addition, Madeline had saved harrowing articles about Gottreich and his sensational development of the procedure that had nearly deprived me of my personality at age eleven. Gottreich had been an ardent disciple of the notorious Dr. Walter Freeman, a passionate advocate of lobotomy, who began experimenting on corpses in 1935 and subsequently developed the elegant procedure known as the transorbital lobotomy. By 1948, Dr. Freeman was performing the procedure on children, professionals, movie stars, including the beautiful and talented Frances Farmer, a radical political activist allegedly in need of the brain-damage cure, along with hundreds of others. By 1955, over 40,000 men, women, and children had undergone "psychosurgery," the name most often used in the popular press for lobotomy.

Doctors had been intrigued by the possibilities of severing or destroying the frontal lobes of troublesome mental patients since the latter half of the nineteenth century. Gottreich's father, Klaus, had also done research on prisoners, children, and mental patients, using an early form of the procedure then called a leucotomy.

Early lobotomies required drilling holes in the patient's skull and inserting instruments or wires into the brain, which sometimes broke off and caused infections or more than the desirable amount of frontal lobe damage. Eventually Freeman and his followers (Gottreich included) found a sturdier tool (an ice pick) and an ingenious new route of entry into the brain (the orbital plate of the skull, directly over the eyeball). The procedure was performed all over the United States in the 1940s and 1950s, most often by psychiatrists and psychologists who had no surgical training whatsoever. The procedure was hailed as "simple, cheap, and miraculous." The only apparent physical side effect (black eyes) was usually remedied by having the patient wear sunglasses for a week or so after the procedure.

The problematic history of the procedure eventually brought dishonor to the house of Gottreich. This family of physicians, once hailed as pioneers in the field of psychosurgery, are now disgraced, along with the procedure they once advocated. No wonder that the citizens of Lewiston stopped calling the old hospital Gottreich Hospital and instead preferred calling it the old Kingdom.

Nobody wanted to remember what happened down in the infamous Pain Room.

"Don't worry, Sally. It's just a name."

THE SALLY DRUSE SUMMIT

Life seldom presents us with exclusively good news, especially when the bearers are doctors or lawyers.

First the good news: According to the results of my blood gas analysis, I was breathing fine. According to my EKG and blood work, I had not had a heart attack. The big question was, of course, had I suffered another seizure? Nobody even bothered to ask me, but the extended EEG I'd had revealed no seizure activity whatsoever. Dr. Massingale was quick to point out that I still could have had a seizure in the elevator the other day, but the most recent EEG did not detect seizure activity or signs of past seizure activity. It wasn't conclusive evidence that I was seizure-free, just suggestive.

The bigger news was that the temporal lobe damage, so much in evidence during my stay in Boston and the probable cause of any seizures I might have had, was now completely resolved. The scans were normal, which was consistent with what Dr. Draper expected, as the kind of contusion and hemorrhage I'd suffered in my right temporal lobe should heal within six to twelve weeks.

The older lesion in the left frontal lobe was also no longer in evidence. Dr. Massingale had a rather convoluted explanation about how and why this could be so, including the different resolutions and angles of the devices, all of which made my eyes glaze. Long and short: no pathology evident on the scans.

As for my hearing, Dr. Massingale went the extra mile for me. I insisted that I had heard the child crying out to me in the shaft of elevator number two. Never mind if the sound itself came from a sensed presence, a voice from the past, myself, my divided self, an angel or a demon. I didn't need to get into that with a medical doctor. I was just trying to convince her that I *heard something* and intended to prove it.

The otologist, Dr. Limen, reported that I had mild, age-related hearing loss and some evidence of tinnitus, which I'd had trouble with before.

I tried to tell Dr. Massingale and Dr. Limen that what I heard in elevator 2 was *not* tinnitus, to which Dr. Limen replied that the sounds "heard" by tinnitus sufferers vary widely, and vary not just from patient to patient but also from time to time in the individual patient. It was entirely possible that several years ago tinnitus caused me to hear buzzing or ringing in my ears, and now, here in 2003, tinnitus was causing me to hear voices in the elevator shafts.

Equally disappointing was the tape: nothing on it but the usual noises one would expect to hear in an elevator shaft — humming, cables racing, air brakes hissing, echoes of same. I pleaded with Dr. Massingale to go one more step up the ladder of tape experts. Would she please give it to one more expert, perhaps in another department? She relented and said she'd try one other doctor of psychoacoustics, but the results so far were near conclusive and negative for any evidence of voices.

Then Dr. Draper and I faced each other across the conference table like Texas Hold 'Em contestants at Binion's World Series of Poker. She didn't have her seizures to crow about, and I didn't have any evidence that I'd heard anything like an actual voice in the elevator. So now what? I knew that Dr. Massingale had a background in psych and had even dabbled in analysis; I sensed that we would now move on to what the odious Stegman had referred to as "the inorganic and the intangible" — or as Bobby would say, was I crackers?

For this delicate series of insinuations, the doctor was at her most charming. Had I entertained the possibility that the voice was the product of what she called "my delightfully fecund imagination"? To her credit, she also offered some astute variations on the possibility that I was "hearing things."

"What if," Dr. Massingale wondered aloud, "the voice originated in your subconscious or a dream state, or some portion of your brain not normally accessible in waking consciousness. A repressed memory, perhaps?" She tried to present it as an alluring psychological phenomenon, instead of a symptom of what she probably feared was really happening; namely, approaching dementia.

The word *repressed* got my attention, because of the Gottreich memories. I had to at least consider that the voice I was hearing was my own: the voice of eleven-year-old Sally Druse, treated by Dr. Gottreich in the Pain Room on the very day of the 1939 fire, a memory too gruesome and horrible to live in the conscious parts of my brain, the long-repressed, spontaneously recovered memory of my own anguish.

As a spiritualist and professional mysterian, I knew of one other esoteric but intriguing possibility: What if my temporal self — bound in time, space, and matter and still equipped with my five earthly senses — had somehow communicated with my immortal soul? If I flew that one by her, she'd probably call in the EEG techs and see if I was having seizure activity. The material brain reels at the concept of a self divided between here and hereafter, but if, as the philosophers tell us, eternity either *is* the now or at the very least *includes* the now, then there is no before and after. I must have one immortal soul, which is capable of at least two modes or channels of being. If death and my bodyless existence after death are merely sides or facets of life, and if death is only the side of life that is hidden from the living, then it's plausible to assume that one could commune with the part of oneself that is immortal and incorporeal.

Thus my unspeakable terror at the sound of this poor child spirit's voice — was it my own? Was I destined for eternal loneliness, desolation, and this unearthly agony of the tortured soul crying out to me from the beyond?

No matter what Dr. Massingale decided, I had no choice but to seek the voice, to continue my investigation until I had an answer. To go on finding and listening to that voice and its inarticulate cries and wait — wait for it to articulate a word in some known language which I would fall upon like a morsel placed before a starveling.

Such pretty-sounding notions.

None of them mattered in the least.

I was discharged and sent home.

If I experienced any more symptoms, Dr. Massingale generously offered to refer me to a psychiatrist.

ABNORMALITIES ARE NORMAL

Over the course of the next week, rumors began making their way outside the hospital about irregularities at the Kingdom. I had to hear about it all from the safety of my easy chair, but I was scheming about how to get back in there and finish my work.

Meanwhile, a team of engineers had raised concerns about the structural integrity of the Kingdom buildings in the wake of the latest focal earthquakes. Other independent engineers and contractors reported freakish disturbances in the machinery and heavy equipment, from elevator malfunctions to heating, ventilation, and air-conditioning breakdowns, artifacts appearing in the scanning devices, and gremlins in the laboratory equipment.

I still knew some patients there on the sunshine ward. Some of them, like Mrs. Kinney, could still tell stories, unlike the staff members, who were all afraid to talk.

The reticence of the KH employees was inspired by an edict from Dr. James (the architect of the infamous Operation Morning Air corporate wellness program), who decreed that it was a termination offense for any KH employee to stage, set, or perpetrate any pranks intended to suggest, directly or indirectly, that Kingdom Hospital was haunted or was the site of paranormal or supernatural activities of any kind, or to discuss or repeat rumors to that effect. Dr. James seemed especially touchy about the employees talking to reporters about the focal earthquakes and aftershocks, probably because they left incontrovertible physical evidence behind that Kingdom Hospital stood on uneasy ground. It's one thing to issue an edict prohibiting discussions of apparitions and ghost doctors roaming the corridors; quite another to spackle over real cracks in the basement corridors and sweat the joints of burst water pipes in the utility chases.

The workplace rules prohibiting discussions of the supernatural came down after the Wellness America hospital chain expressed a keen interest in acquiring "the Kingdom" as an expansion property. The Kingdom's lawyers told the hospital's board that a seller has a legal duty to disclose the existence of any defects in the condition of the premises, no matter how baffling or inexplicable. When the Wellness America lawyers and investment bankers began doing due diligence and routine inspections, they soon discovered what I felt the first time I stepped into the lobby: Kingdom Hospital is not well. The scientists, specialists, and engineers attributed the ongoing disturbances recorded there to constructional imperfections, faulty feng shui, shifts in tectonic plates, or even sick building syndrome (a diagnosis no sane hospital administrator would embrace). However, the patients, the staff, even the visitors sensed that the premature signs of decay, the disruptions and equipment malfunctions, had more mysterious and frightening origins. If Kingdom Hospital was sick, its illness was what the physicians call an idiopathy, a disease arising from an obscure or unknown cause.

The hospital's public relations consultants did a superb job of managing information by issuing only the most strategic communications about persistent rumors of oddities on the premises of southern Maine's largest and newest research hospital. The local newspaper and Kingdom Hospital shared more than a few board members, so the news accounts were extremely deferential to the reputation of the Kingdom. At most, the local coverage featured restrained accounts of focal earthquakes and minor structural infirmities.

In their defense, the experts who explained away the unusual tremors with formulas and stress tests did not set out to deceive the public about the disturbing problems at Kingdom Hospital. Worse: They first deceived themselves, so that by the time they faced the reporters, they spoke their false words with pure hearts. They used intricate theories about oscillons, modal analyses, neotectonics, and focal seismicity to explain how an earthquake could damage a single complex of buildings and go almost unnoticed in the surrounding community. Not to misinform, but because science offered the only explanation that would allow the patients and staff to sleep at night.

Questions persisted, and people continued asking them. It was around this time that Dr. James famously remarked to a *Sun Journal* reporter, "Don't worry, the abnormalities are normal," a proclamation for which he was roundly and justifiably mocked by the staff.

Like the proverbial drunk who lost his keys in a dark alley and then searched for them a block away under the streetlamp because the light was better there, the doctors, Ph.D.s, and engineers who investigated the disquieting aberrations at the Kingdom looked for explanations only where reason and science cast their lucid beams. If the shadows concealed more ominous and enigmatic disruptions in nature, the scientists weren't interested, because apparitions and phantasms by definition do not generate data that are conducive to testing and confirmation using the scientific method.

THE NOTE

I holed up at home and waited for a chance to

return to the Kingdom, resume my investigation, and reach the child, if I could. Even as children, Maddy and I had believed that if we only knew the little girl's name and what had happened to her, we could help her. But I also knew that if I tried to readmit myself to the Kingdom too soon, it would raise flags. Besides, my complaint would be what exactly? Seizures? Then I'd have to take those deadly anti-sparkle pills again, which would sap me of the mental energy I needed to investigate and to deal with the likes of Dr. Rat if he came around again.

While I waited, I went through Madeline's papers and clippings, and so it was on one bitter cold afternoon in February, the sky a tattletale gray and the wind making the leaded windowpanes hum in the casements, that I found what the police and the health care workers at the Kingdom had called Madeline's "suicide note."

Ollie and Danny were right. Madeline hadn't left a note per se. She must have indeed pursued writing, as a hobby at least, because the pages looked like a term paper laid out in neatly formatted text and indented paragraphs. Some other wretch at rope's end tells the cruel world good-bye with a pencil and a scrap of paper, but a writer needs a computer and a laser printer and 10,000 words to get the job done. I had gone through the papers and clippings before looking for handwritten notes and thought Hilda must have held the "suicide note" back.

Truth be told, Madeline had simply kept a

careful journal. At the end, her thoughts, of course, turned to suicide, so she wrote about it. It's a natural thing for nervous, creative types. The pages that were open on the table when Madeline decided to take the final leap into the night must have mentioned suicide. When the cops find papers discussing suicide and a body with its head in the oven, they call the papers a suicide note.

Madeline addressed most of her last remarks to Hilda, including warnings that the Gottreich materials should not be given to anyone, especially not to me.

I found the sections referencing me that Ray had copied for Bobby: "God has blessed Sally Druse with a memory more merciful than mine. I will not disturb her peace with cruel remembrance." Elsewhere, Madeline discussed her careful decision not to reacquaint me with our mutual horror, despite her lifelong suffering and despite being haunted by those same memories she had so selflessly spared me. In truth, Ray missed copying other passages that mentioned me, but so far at least, they told me nothing that I hadn't surmised on my own.

Then, unfortunately, I found those portions of Madeline's journal that Ray must have been referring to when he said that the papers were "too disturbing" to give to anyone.

It couldn't be worse, could it?

It was, for different reasons. Guilt. And the guilt was mine for what I'd done to Peggy

Kruger. In her papers, Madeline described the misfortune that had befallen her daughter, Peggy, the one I'd spoken to on the phone, the one who Bobby said was a feeb and had so feverishly tried to hurt herself when she'd looked through Madeline's papers.

Peggy Kruger had married in June of 1993, relatively advanced in her childbearing years; she was thirty-eight at the time. Peggy had been worried about the biological clock, but she must have sneaked in under the wire, because she was soon a happily married, expectant mother, living in Lewiston and going in for prenatal care to the Kingdom Hospital maternity clinics. She was married to a local agent for a national securities firm, which was just coming into the salad days of the nineties stock boom. They had a bungalow not far from Madeline's, and Grandma was eagerly awaiting a new granddaughter.

In mid-1994, during the ninth month of her pregnancy, at about ten o'clock one August evening, Peggy's contractions increased and her cervix began dilating, so her husband drove her to Kingdom Hospital for the delivery.

I should mention that, after perusing the rest of Madeline's papers, it was clear to me that Madeline had not been back to the new Kingdom Hospital since the old one had burned down. She was probably in no hurry to go there and disturb the cruel roots of memory. But based upon her description of the events,

Madeline knew her daughter would deliver the child at Kingdom Hospital, and Grandma was not the least bit concerned. Madeline had no reason to believe that Gottreich was anything but dead.

I started shaking uncontrollably as I read the description of events. How the Evil had touched Madeline, then touched her daughter, and indeed it would seem pursued poor Madeline until she fairly leaped to her own death.

Poor Peggy had a difficult labor interspersed by periods of fitful sleep fraught with nightmares. In the morning, her child, a little girl, was delivered stillborn. Tragedy enough for any woman to bear.

Then Peggy related the following to Madeline. While still in labor and during one of her erratic respites of sleep, Peggy had a graphic, terrifying nightmare. She told Madeline that she dreamed she was in a church with her newborn baby. The child was in her christening clothes, dressed in radiant white, awaiting baptism. Suddenly Peggy heard blasts from the organ in the choir loft. A pipe organ booming out a dirge, which made the very pews shake and the flagstones vibrate under her feet.

Peggy dreamed that out in the churchyard, a grave yawned open, and an old man dressed in tattered black clothes rose out of the earth. He was bald, with a hideous livid scar running the length of his skull-like head. He rushed into the church and tore the child from her arms.

The deafening music made it impossible for anyone to hear Peggy's cries for help. She chased the hideous old man back out to the churchyard, where she saw him carry the infant to the grave.

She stood by helplessly and watched as the earth closed over them both forever.

The music stopped. Peggy awoke, and the next morning —

A few years later, Peggy happened to look over Madeline's shoulder while her mom was going through papers and files. Peggy pointed to the photo of Dr. Ebenezer Gottreich and cried out in speechless recognition.

I shook all over, blessed myself, and clutched at the crucifix on my necklace and my crystal. The true horror was imagining poor Madeline, thinking she had made a clean getaway from the horrors of this world, instead waking up in Kingdom Hospital, knowing that Gottreich still roamed there.

God never leaves us alone with such horror and desolation. He is always with us. Our faith tells us that. It's true I could no longer look at those wrenching passages of Madeline's papers, but another batch caught my eye, because I saw that it was captioned: "The Little Girl."

In it, Madeline described how the little girl had saved everyone in the old hospital by ringing her bell the day of the fire in 1939. How Madeline hoped that the little girl had finally found rest. How Maddy and I had asked the little girl to tell us her name, but she was too afraid of us to let us help her.

Then a series of passages, wherein Madeline described how as little Maddy Kruger with the whooping cough in the Old Kingdom Hospital, she had tried to reach the little girl.

Maddy's grandmother had fallen seriously ill and had been confined at the old hospital during the same time that we had been treated there for whooping cough. As I read Maddy's descriptions, I seemed to remember the old lady. She'd had consumption and smelled of ashes and wax, as if she was already in a coffin. Like us, the old lady had a bad cough, but hers was different. She was old, and her disease had earned its name by consuming people.

Maddy's grandma was going to die. Soon.

But before she did, Madeline told the old woman about the little girl. How Maddy had never heard a cry from anyone, living or dead, that was so sad. Maddy's grandmother must have been a true believer in the world of the spirits, because she told Maddy that she would look for the little girl when she passed through the valley that separates this life from the next. Her grandma told Maddy to bring a candle to her bedside at the hour of her death, and the old lady would show her how to reach the little girl's spirit.

Madeline described the session at some length. When the life was almost out of her grandma, the old lady told her to light the candle. Then she held Maddy's hand and said, "I'll be in the borderlands for only a very short time. A radiant light will appear and I'll be drawn toward it. But for a few seconds, I will be in between. If the little girl is lost there and if I find her, I will try to lead her to the light. If I find the little girl, I will blow the candle flame and make it stutter for you. If I can get her to follow me to the light, I'll blow it twice."

I almost wept imagining little Maddy bravely holding her grandmama's hand, eagerly watching the candle flame for some sign that the little girl had found rest. According to Maddy's notes, she was talking to her grandma after she'd died.

"Did you find her? Did you find the little girl, Grandma?"

The flame guttered and blew sideways.

"Yes, oh, that's good," Maddy had said. "Can you show her the light? Can you show her how to cross over and find rest?"

The poor child stared at the candle and waited until the nurse came in and led her away.

Her grandma was gone and the little girl still lost. Her grandma had warned her that this might happen, because the light is magnetic and it pulls you into its divine warmth. Confused and frightened spirits can't find it. They get lost in between in the First State after death, with no one to help them.

When I finished reading this passage, I felt as

if someone had touched a bare electrical cord somewhere at the base of my spine.

I sat bolt upright, looked out the window, and cried, "Lenny!"

THE RETURN OF EVIL

ANOTHER LITTLE GIRL

The next morning, I was sitting at my window with the paper, sipping my tea, wondering how I was going to get back in to see poor dear Lenny. I'd called in to check on him, and Brick Bannerman reported that he was barely conscious, fading in and out — more out than in, lately. His primary physician was Dr. Louis Traff, who was not about to grant me permission to visit, and Lenny was not alert enough to do so himself. So I was momentarily bereft. He could go at any time, and I had to be there for that. We were soulmates, lovers, never mind that we didn't have papers recognized by the police. I also needed to reach the little girl again by riding elevator 2 to the sunshine ward. She'd cried out to me how many times now? But she hadn't found the courage to use words. I needed to know her name, needed to know the circumstances of her death, why and how she came to be lost in the land between, where darkness is the only light.

Bobby was late, and I was just starting to think he must have put in to work a double for the overtime, something he wouldn't normally do. He'd just bought a new computer last month, which meant he was done with discretionary consumer spending for another two years at least, and I couldn't imagine him working overtime to save for anything else. Sure enough, fifteen minutes later he pulled his pickup into the garage and came in looking more harried than usual.

"You're late. Did you go out for some breakfast with Ollie and Danny?"

"No, Mum. It was hell night at the Kingdom."

"What happened, Bobby?"

"Another earthquake, for starters," he said. "Then the usual business hauling people here and there and cleaning up again."

"I didn't feel any earthquakes," I said. "You know I'm a light sleeper. I didn't feel one the night Madeline died either, Bobby. How is that?"

"They call them focal earthquakes. They don't affect the surrounding structures," he said. "They have some seismologist coming in from Berkeley to measure them and see if anything can be done about them."

I sat up and paid attention in a hurry.

"So it's a peculiar sort of earthquake, is it, Bobby? As in it only affects the hospital? What else happened? Any medical emergencies? Any little girls get in trouble?"

His mouth fell open like an unhinged gate.

"Who did you talk to, Mum? Did you call Brick Bannerman this morning? Did she tell you about the trouble with the little girl in the operating room?"

I was up and out of my chair and gathering my things.

"What? Mum? What are you doing?"

"I'm going to the hospital, Bobby. It'll take me just a few minutes to pack."

"Pack?"

"I'm checking back in," I said. "I'm feeling quite poorly. Very poorly. I'm pins and needles all up and down my left arm. Prickling sensations, stabbing pains. It could be the early symptoms of another seizure."

"You don't have seizures, Mum. Remember? You're clean. You checked out. Your scans are normal. There's nothing there to cause seizures any more. I think they gave up on you, Mum. They just think you're daffy, not an epileptic."

"Well, then I'm being admitted for daffiness and for tingling in my extremities. Bobby, it could be MS, for goodness sake. I'm still young, it could ruin the rest of my life."

MONA KLINGERMAN

Bobby drove me to the Kingdom and filled me in on some of the particulars, although he hadn't paid all that much attention to the details of yet another medical tragedy coming down the assembly line. A neurosurgeon, one of the recruits they'd brought in to staff the new neurosciences division, had performed emergency surgery on a little girl during the night. A Mona Klingerman. I knew the name because Renee Klingerman came from money and had been in the *Sun Journal* society pages, usually being recognized for her efforts at volunteering for various worthy causes. Now poor little Mona wasn't quite waking up on cue, and the physicians were warning of various "deficits," possibly permanent ones.

Bobby said the earthquake occurred during or shortly after the procedure, and that he and Otto had spent the rest of the shift downstairs cleaning up after it.

When I got to admitting, I was seen by a new doctor (fresh meat!), Christine Draper. I told her I'd been bothered for almost a week by a prickling sensation in my left hand and forearm — an annoying tingling, as if my arm had fallen asleep, then had never fully awakened and was stuck in some hypnopompic purgatory for accursed aged limbs. I also told her that I'd had an episode of vertigo. Several, and this time I almost pulled the refrigerator over on top of me. I made a pinch out of my index finger and thumb and told her I'd come *this close* to shattering my hip. Also, heart palpitations, skipped beats, chest pains.

Dr. Draper apparently heard enough. She admitted me for testing. I was ordered on bed rest because of intermittent vertigo, and she ordered some tests to rule out multiple sclerosis, Guillain-Barré syndrome, and other sensory neuropathies. She also ordered an MRI of my head, just to make sure that she wasn't seeing new fallout from my previous head trauma.

After the MRI, I went to find Lenny on the sunshine ward.

Poor dear, he was nearly unresponsive. I smoothed his brow and whispered in his ear, telling him I would be there for him. I telephoned Bobby and told him to get to a florist and find me a nice big bag of rose petals, because if Lenny should suddenly take a turn for the worse, I wanted to be ready. We could keep them in the refrigerator up here if we had to.

I knew several of the other patients on the ward from my days as a volunteer, including Mrs. Eileen Kinney, a delightful woman with end-stage ovarian cancer. Eileen knew her Swedenborg like nobody's business. She said that reading his descriptions of heaven were for her like reading a travelogue about a wonderful vacation spot where she'd already lived as a local.

She and I drew several of the others together around Lenny's bed and began praying and meditating on the lives of those who had already gone before us. I decided that it was worth trying to contact any spirits that might be present. So I drew the shades and darkened the lights. Eileen and I began opening the lines of communication, in hopes of discovering a presence.

I felt Eileen's hand twitch as I sensed what she also felt: Something cold and quite nearly reptilian was very near and approaching rapidly, a spiritual predator of some kind wearing the mark of the beast, no doubt. As he drew closer, I clutched my druse crystal and cried out.

I was certain it was Gottreich we would all be contending with soon. Dr. Rat with more Warfarin or a fresh ice pick, or on the prowl for another defenseless infant.

I couldn't help but announce the presence to the others. "He's getting closer. He has big blond hair. He's tall. Ugly. Lost in his inner darkness. A terrible man! He means me harm."

I gasped for air. I heard the presence at the door, angry, loud, abusive, full of hatred and wrath.

THE BEAST

What came through the door left me winded and near circulatory shock. I again had the feeling that I was already dead and had fallen through the cracks to hell. Was I in Boston again? Sally Druse, are you so old and daffy that you can't keep your infernal hospitals straight?

It was none other than the odious Dr. Stegman, he of Boston General Hospital, of which he had spoken so haughtily to me about. Almost a year ago? More? But how? Why? What diabolical confluence of malignant tides had washed him up on our shores? And why an entourage of physicians, including Dr. Hook and Dr. Draper, along with nurse Brick Bannerman? Again he swaggered out front, barking orders, just as he had in Boston.

I almost asked him. *Dr. Stegman, didn't you once tell me that I would never find the likes of you in Lewisport? What are you doing in Maine, which is medically speaking nowhere near Boston, Massachusetts?*

I had a feeling that it might have something to do with a fall from grace accelerated by a good plaintiffs' lawyer. I saw him glare at the others, so I promptly took full responsibility for the prayer circle.

He glared right back at me, and asked Brick, "Is this one Druse?"

The beast had forgotten me! I should have expected it. I had once been "interesting"; then I had been defined and billed and sent on my way. Now I was just another old biddy for him to vent his poisonous spleen upon.

As the drama unfolded, I learned that he was indeed in charge and that he was wroth to the point of apoplexy because new protocols, instituted by his highness, had been ignored, to wit: Dr. Draper had ordered an expensive new MRI scan of my noggin, without clearing the order through Stegman's office. Furthermore, Stegman made it clear that the request would not have been approved because of my allegedly vague symptoms. He displayed the scan to everyone present and railed aloud about how it showed absolutely nothing in the way of abnormalities, as if only scans that found malignant brain tumors were worth doing. Then he turned the full measure of his ire on Dr. Hook, who, I later learned, had pretended that he'd ordered the scan to protect his lady, Dr. Draper, from Mussolini.

I was dressed down in front of everyone, called a malingerer, and threatened. Then the beast ordered Dr. Hook to discharge me as soon as possible.

By the time he left, I realized that life is indeed a dream, where personas shift shapes, assume roles, and trade guises without changing the essence of their natures. Stegman was a protégé, if not the heir apparent, to Gottreich.

None of us could breathe regularly until he was gone. We had to wait for Evil to pass before we dared speak.

Someone had alerted Bobby to the goings-on and he showed up later, bearing an envelope.

"Mum, I never did give you that letter from your friend Claudia. Now she sent a second one, and this one is marked URGENT."

I nodded and sighed.

"Bobby, I think I know what's in Claudia's letters. I'll read them at home."

SOUND ANALYSIS

There seemed nothing for me to do but pack my things. That's just what I was doing when Dr. Draper stopped by to say good-bye and to apologize for the beast's deportment. Apparently Stegman was one of the neuro-gurus the Kingdom had recruited to staff their expanded new neurosciences division. I also had the temerity to ask if he happened to be the surgeon who had operated on Mona Klingerman the night previous.

I didn't have to ask, but I did. Innocence victimized again by the cruelty of science, and the little girl had come back screaming earthquakes again. The child was now my ally, and from here on out, we had two mortal adversaries: one lurking in the land between life and death, and another here in the real world. The old Kingdom and the new.

But there was something else. A delightful surprise.

Dr. Draper said that Dr. Massingale had asked a favor of her — namely, to convey me to see an experimental psychologist, a Ph.D. in psychoacoustics, Dr. Jeremiah Duling, who had been pleased to examine my hearing tests and the tape I'd made that fateful day in the elevator and would be further pleased to meet with me and discuss his findings. I think the doctors were all feeling a little sorry for me, now that word had got around about the treatment I'd received from Stegman.

Dr. Duling had heard that I was wondering if perhaps the sounds that I had tried to tape did not occupy the spectrum audible to the normal human ear. He had sent word to Dr. Massingale that the situation was far more complicated and needed explaining.

En route, Dr. Draper told me how, over and above audiology and otology, they now had a new department of neuropsychology, complete with doctors who study psychoacoustics and neuro-audiology. All part of the grand new expansion.

She also warned me that Dr. Duling was something of a pure scientist, and that it was entirely possible that neither one of us would come away with any understanding of what he'd said to us, unless I happened to have an advanced degree in psychoacoustics.

"Is he more open-minded than those flat-landers you sent me to in otology?" I asked.

She answered my question by showing me into Dr. Duling's office, where I saw a large rumpled man behind a large messy desk flanked by what looked a triptych of flat-panel computer monitors.

After introductions, he almost never looked at us. Instead he seemed to be pulling documents or files up on the screens in front of him and peering into them — an odd sensation for us, because we could see only the backs of the monitors and his brow furrowing as he studied them.

I almost announced that there were human beings present, but I let Dr. Draper run the show instead.

"The patient has mild age-related hearing loss," said Duling. "While overall hearing diminishes with age, there is a well-known effect of broadening in the bandwidth of hearing in the elderly, resulting in better temporal resolution. To be precise, better temporal fine structure discrimination."

"Ooo-kay," said Dr. Draper.

I could see by the look on her face that Dr. Draper understood no more of it than I did. But I was all ears anyway and had a good feeling about it.

"Are there lay terms that might convey what you just said?" asked Dr. Draper.

Duling glanced up and barked, "Because she's *old* she may hear stuff in complex sounds that normal people can't hear. How's that?"

"Yes," said Draper. "Good."

I nodded and kept my thoughts to myself: *Of course I hear stuff in complex sounds that normal people don't hear. I'm clairaudient, for God's sake.*

"She also has a history of tinnitus," said Duling. "Not a problem for us in deciphering the tape. Like everyone else, she sometimes exhibits the well-known phenomena of OAEs, otoacoustic emissions."

Dr. Draper's eyes opened a little wider, but Duling didn't notice.

"They were discovered about ten or twenty

years ago," said Duling. "Her ears, our ears, in the proper circumstances actually emit very low-level sound, not just spontaneously, but these can also be *evoked* in response to external acoustic stimulation."

"Again, the lay terms might be helpful," she said.

"How shall I put this," said Duling. "In some circumstances, using the proper sensitive equipment, it is possible for scientists like me to *hear the ringing in your ears!* How does that grab you?"

"How exciting!" I said.

"I'm glad someone's impressed," he said. "Now, all of this would be moot when it comes to the particular tape you made in the elevator, except for one fortuitous accident. When you had your episode or fainting spell, your recording device landed literally millimeters from your ear."

"That's what Bobby said!" I could barely contain myself. "I don't know why. I don't think I did it on purpose."

"So," he continued, "I examined the tape for very faint echoes of the sounds actually heard by your ear, as those very faint sounds otoacoustically echoed back into your recording device. To be clear, these are sounds *you* hear because age has endowed you with superior temporal fine structure discrimination. Us youngsters can't hear them, which means we can't echo back those sounds the way your ear does. But us youngsters *can* hear the very faint echoes of what *you* heard if those echoes got captured on the tape. Got it?"

Even Dr. Draper was on the edge of her chair now.

"So what I did," he continued, "was take your tape, especially the end of it, and perform what we call fine grain analysis. We strip away extraneous noises one by one. We do signal averaging and we gradually dig the signal out of the noise."

"Uh, how about some more lay termi—" began Dr. Draper.

"Naw," said Duling, "I'll just play it for you. Is this what you heard?"

He clicked his mouse and stared into his computer screen, and miracles and wonders, I heard the poor child's voice. Crying. Calling out to us from beyond the grave. I was gooseflesh head to toe.

"There's more distortion than I'd like," he said, "but is that it?"

Dr. Draper was white, for the forlorn voice affected her the way it did me when I first heard it.

"This is —" she began.

"Kinda creepy if you ask me," said Duling.

CONTACT

LENNY

By the time I got to Lenny's bedside, it was night. Late. A winter storm was breaking outside. Lenny was rousing himself to moments of lucidity, but his breathing was failing fast. I was able to ask for his help and explain what needed to be done in the moments immediately following death.

I was a woman on a mission until I stopped and reminded myself to *be* in the moment, even though the moment was fraught with so much life. And death.

"Lenny," I said, "here we are at the end. My sweet, handsome lover."

I kissed his cheek and rubbed eucalyptus and spearmint oils on his scaly old skin. That made him smile. I knew he was still with me.

One more time, for the ages.

The sunshine ward was quiet, except for the soft beep of his morphine pump and snow blowing softly against the windows.

He turned his head to one side, almost as if Lenny the warrior didn't want an old woman to see his face just now.

"Is that you, Sally?"

"Yes, Lenny," I said. "I'm here."

"Where have you been all my life, Sally?"

He chuckled, but I saw a tear bead up in the corner of one eye.

"I've been ghost-hunting, Lenny."

He laughed. "You and your ghosts."

"Yes," I said, "Sally and her ghosts."

"How I loved you, Sally. You and all your crazy ghosts."

"All my crazy ghosts," I said.

I started covering him with rose petals. Combing his white hair. Touching his body tenderly, while he could still feel me.

"You want to do it in a chair again, Sally?"

Still had his sense of humor, but his breathing was agonal, coming and going in fits, punctuated by alarming episodes of complete stillness, during which I was afraid that he'd already gone.

"Only the once," I whispered.

"Only the once," he said, "but it was for the ages."

I felt a single tremor rumble through the building.

I'd used all the petals, covered him in them.

"This is the big one, isn't it?" he asked. "Those Japs couldn't kill me, but now here I am, all broke down."

"Are you afraid, Lenny?"

He smiled. "A little."

"Don't be. You're just passing over to all those crazy ghosts. I'll be coming soon; I'm an old biddy myself."

"Sally . . . do you hear a bell?"

I listened, and indeed I could hear the girl's bell, ringing ever so faintly.

"You still want me to find the little girl for you?" he said.

"Yes," I said.

His mouth fell open, and he was still.

"Lenny?"

He smiled again, and his diaphragm jerked and drew in one spasmodic breath.

I pulled out my candle and set it on the tray table next to us.

"Lenny, remember what I told you about the candle. When you pass over, you'll be in the First State after death, a space you must cross over to reach the light. If I'm right, the little girl I'm looking for is there. She hasn't gone on, and I don't know why. I don't even know her name. You'll see a light — a lovely bright light. You'll want to go into it. But don't! Not right away! Call for the little girl! Linger in Swedenborgian space, Lenny. Put her in touch with me. Tell her to blow the candle if she hears me. She won't let you lead her to the light, but tell her I want to help her if she will let me. I feel we are sisters outside of time in some way that I don't fully understand yet. Tell her I must know her name. I must find out what happened to her."

Lenny's jaw dropped and he fell completely still.

I lifted his hand and kissed it, felt tears on my cheeks.

"Lenny, are you still there?"

Nothing. Then the candle blew sideways.

I was all plucked gooseflesh, shaking with excitement.

"Lenny, is she there, Lenny? Is the little girl there?"

Again the candle guttered and shot sideways.

"Do you see my little girl, Lenny?"

Yes, said the flame.

"Can you speak to her?"

A long second or two of nothing. I knew the time couldn't last, Lenny would pass over any second.

"Lenny, ask her to blow the candle twice if she can hear me. Please, Lenny?"

The darkness seemed to open at my feet into a dark chasm separating here from hereafter. A long silence, then the candle guttered once, then again.

Time stood still the moment I saw the second fluctuation of the flame. I had made contact with the little girl, a spirit in the beyond, the voice that I had heard in my travels in the borderlands.

"My child, I know you can hear me. And you know I can hear you. We're sisters in some way. I know it."

I stared into the candle flame.

"Can you still hear me?"

The flame was blown sideways, as if a living person blew across it.

"Child, in death we cross over to the light, where we rediscover all the moments of our past life and freely combine them in eternal dreams. But I fear that your dream is a terrible nightmare, my child, and so you cannot cross over into the light. I so want to help you, dear. But I can't help until I know what happened. Can you tell me? Can you tell me what happened to you?"

The candle guttered sideways again, as in reply.

"Yes? Oh, my dear. Who hurt you? Was it one sworn to heal? Is that why you haunt these halls? Was it a doctor?"

Whoosh, the flame was blown violently and completely out. A glass broke and I felt a cold aura pass through the room. A gust of Evil that made me tremble.

I looked around for the thing, but all I could hear was laughter, the malicious spirit of a young boy from the sound of the voice.

"I command the other spirit to leave us. Leave us in peace. I'm not afraid of you! Why won't you let me talk to the girl? Why do you interfere? Leave us in peace!"

I heard more wicked laughter reverberate. Then the pitiful cries of the child tore holes in my heart.

The Evil One said, "Hail, Mary, full of disgrace. The Lord has abandoned thee. The Lord has abandoned little Mary in the valley in between."

"Mary?" I said, and I heard her cries anguishing the night. "Mary, is that your name?"

I lit the candle. It seemed to gutter momentarily, then stabilized.

"Mary, is that your name, child? Is it Mary?"

A gentle breath blew across the flame. One time.

"Don't listen to Evil, my child. I won't abandon you, and neither will the Lord. I'll help you, Mary. Look at us! We hear each other. Your voice is real. I can hear it. I'll soon know what happened to you and how you were lost."

For one instant I stood outside of time, much the way one does in the textbook mystical experience. I saw time as both particles and waves, a vast collection of individual seconds, innumerable as water molecules in all the oceans of the earth, and also saw it as a single undivided eternal moment, a moving image of eternity.

I knew the child was crying out from beyond the grave against the crimes of science. Against the suffering of the innocents. Against the pain of the few in the name of the greater good. Evil will always be with us, but you and I, Mary, will make our stand against it in the here and now, in the faraway past, and the life yet to come. Before our work is done, we may have to journey even farther back in time, to the place where Evil touched you, my dear.

"I promise you this, Mary, you shall not go alone."

THE END

Eleanor Druse
2 November 2003
Lewiston, Maine